Praise for
M. C. Beaton's Acclaimed
HAMISH MACBETH MYSTERIES

"Longing for escape? Tired of waiting for Brigadoon to materialize? Time for a trip to Lochdubh, the scenic, if somnolent, village in the Scottish Highlands where M. C. Beaton sets her beguiling whodunits featuring Constable Hamish Macbeth."
    —*New York Times Book Review*

"With residents and a constable so authentic it won't be long before tourists will be seeking Lochdubh and believing in the reality of Hamish Macbeth as surely as they believed in Sherlock Holmes."
    —*Denver Rocky Mountain News*

"Macbeth is the sort of character who slyly grows on you."
    —*Chicago Sun-Times*

"For those who like th_____a-
ton the rose-colored gl_____"
    —*Pl*

"The Hamish Macbet_____p
away from our hectic world."
    —*Fredericksburg Free Lance-Star* (VA)

"The detective novels of M. C. Beaton, a master of outrageous black comedy . . . have reached cult status in the United States."
    —*Times Magazine* (London)

"On a scale of one to ten, M. C. Beaton's Constable Hamish Macbeth merits a ten plus."
    —*Buffalo News*

Previous Hamish Macbeth Mysteries by M. C. Beaton

M. C. BEATON

Death *of a* Prankster

GC

GRAND CENTRAL
PUBLISHING

NEW YORK   BOSTON

Copyright © 1992 by M. C. Beaton
Excerpt from *Death of a Kingfisher* copyright © 2012 by Marion Chesney
All rights reserved. In accordance with the U.S. Copyright Act of 1976, the scanning, uploading, and electronic sharing of any part of this book without the permission of the publisher is unlawful piracy and theft of the author's intellectual property. If you would like to use material from the book (other than for review purposes), prior written permission must be obtained by contacting the publisher at permissions@hbgusa.com. Thank you for your support of the author's rights.

Grand Central Publishing
Hachette Book Group
237 Park Avenue
New York, NY 10017
www.HachetteBookGroup.com

Grand Central Publishing is a division of Hachette Book Group, Inc.
The Grand Central Publishing name and logo is a trademark of Hachette Book Group, Inc.

The Hachette Speakers Bureau provides a wide range of authors for speaking events. To find out more, go to www.hachettespeakersbureau.com or call (866) 376-6591.

The publisher is not responsible for websites (or their content) that are not owned by the publisher.

Printed in the United States of America

This edition published by arrangement with St. Martin's Press.

First Grand Central Publishing mass market edition: June 2012

10 9 8 7 6 5 4 3 2 1

OPM

For my good neighbours,
Jean and Oliver Dicks, and their
daughter, Kate. With love.

Chapter One

Full well they laugh'd, with counterfeited glee,
At all his jokes, for many a joke had he

—Oliver Goldsmith

Money, or the prospect of it, makes hope spring eternal, and so that was probably the reason a small group of people were packing their bags to travel to the very north of Britain to stay with Mr. Trent.

Without that lure of money, it was doubtful whether any of them would have decided to go. But Mr. Andrew Trent had written to his relatives to say that he did not have long to live. Mr. Trent was a practical joker and, although in his eighties, age had not dimmed his zest for the apple-pie bed or the whoopee cushion. He was a widower, his wife having died some twenty years before, driven to her grave, said his relatives, by her husband's relentless jokes. His home, Arrat House, outside the village of Arrat in Sutherland, was difficult to get to. The thought of his practical jokes made all his relatives shudder. Possibly that was the reason they all lived in the south of England, as far away from the old man as they could get. But now he said he was dying, and with all that money at stake, the long journey and the prospect of an uncomfortable and possibly humiliating stay must be faced. Of course, the old man could be joking . . .

"I'll kill him if he is," said his daughter Angela. Angela prided herself on plain-speaking. She was a tall, ungainly woman with iron-grey hair and an incipient moustache. She wore mannish clothes and had a booming voice. She and her sister Betty were both in their fifties. They had never married, although both had been fairly good-looking in their youth. Rumour had it that their father's dreadful jokes had driven any prospective suitors away. They lived together in London, as they had done for quite some time, and detested each other but were bound to each other by rivalry and habit. Betty was small and quiet and affected a certain shy timidity but seemed expert at coming out with sharp and wounding remarks.

"You're always saying that," said Betty, "and yet when you see him, you positively *cringe*."

"No, I don't. Stop being spiteful. Have you seen my long underwear?"

"You won't need it. Dad has good central heating."

"Pah!" said Angela, finding and holding up a long pair of woollen underpants. "You don't think I'm going to stay locked up in that house with him all day long. I want to get out and take some brisk walks. Do you think he's really ill?"

Betty put her head on one side and pursed her lips. "Good chance. The writing was shaky, not like his usual style."

"Then that's that," said Angela. "Can't risk not going. What if he left it all to that wimp of a son of his?"

The wimp referred to was Mr. Trent's adopted son Charles. He was in his late twenties, a very beautiful man with golden curls, blue eyes and an athlete's body. His short life of failure did not seem to have affected his sunny good nature. He had done comparatively well at school, but everything had gone downhill from then on. He had lasted only one term at Oxford University before dropping out. After that, he had drifted from one job to the other. He always plunged into each job with great enthusiasm, an enthusiasm which only lasted a few months. He had been a photographer, an insurance salesman, an advertising copy-writer, among other things, and was now selling Lifehanz vitamins to shops around the country. He too was packing, while his fiancée, Titchy Gold, dithered about his studio flat in bra and panties. Titchy Gold was assumed to be a stage name, although she protested in a wide-eyed way that she had been christened that name by her parents, who had been Shakespearian actors, although what that had to do with it nobody knew, the great Bard not having run to names like Titchy. She was a television actress, currently playing the part of a floozie in a popular crime series. Marilyn Monroe was her idol, and as Titchy was blonde and busty, she did her best to look like her.

Charles had read his father's letter out to her. "Is he really very rich?" asked Titchy.

"Rolling in it," said Charles. "Masses and masses of dosh, lolly and gelt, my sweet."

"He'll leave it to you," said Titchy. "Bound to. You're his son. He'll probably fall for me. Old men always do."

"I don't know," said Charles. "He really despises me. Says I'm shiftless. Might leave it to his brother."

Mr. Andrew Trent's brother Jeffrey, a stockbroker, was a thin, spare, fastidious man. He was fifteen years younger than his brother, and his wife, Jan, was twenty years younger than he, a second marriage, Jeffrey having divorced the first Mrs. Trent. Jan was a cool, elegant, bitchy woman. "He's got to die sometime," said Jan. "I mean, living up there is enough to kill anyone. Do you think he'll leave you anything? I mean, he must, surely."

"He might leave it all to Charles."

"He won't," said Jan firmly. "He loathes that boy.

Now Paul is a different matter. I told Paul to pack his bags and report to the bedside."

"He won't leave Paul anything," exclaimed Jeffrey.

"He might," said Jan. "Paul is everything Charles is not." Paul was her son by her first marriage.

A day later, Paul was standing in front of the departure board at King's Cross station waiting to board the train to Inverness. He was an owlish young man of twenty-five who was a research assistant at some atomic establishment in Surrey. He was very precise and correct, three-piece suit and horn-rimmed glasses. His mother did not know he was bringing a girl-friend with him, which was just as well because Melissa Clarke was just the sort of girl the chilly Jan could be guaranteed to loathe. Her appearance was vaguely punk—black leather jacket and trousers, heavy white make-up, purple eye-shadow, white lips, and earrings that looked like instruments of torture. She was awed at the idea of a country-house visit and so had a slight sneer on her face which she hoped disguised the fact that she felt extremely gauche and wished she had worn more conventional clothes. Also her hair was dyed bright pink, hacked in shreds and backcombed. She worked with Paul in the research establishment. She had not even known he fancied her. This peculiar trip north was their first date.

He had marched up to her in the lab, sweating

lightly, and had simply asked her if she could get leave and come with him. Intrigued, she had accepted. She liked Paul. He had only seen her before in sensible blouse and skirt and white lab coat. She had reverted to the fashion of her student days for the journey. She cursed that camp hairdresser who had talked her into the pink fright which was what was left of her once thick and glossy brown hair. She felt near to tears and wanted to run away and the only thing that stopped her running was the fact that Paul appeared genuinely grateful for her support and did not even seem to have noticed her new appearance.

"You must be very fond of him," she volunteered.

"Who?" asked Paul vaguely.

"Why, Mr. Trent, the one we're going to visit," said Melissa.

"Oh, him! I hate him. I hope he's dead when we get there. I'm only going to please my mother. She's going, of course."

"Your mother!" squeaked Melissa in alarm. "You didn't say anything about your mother. My God, why didn't you *tell* me?"

"There's our train," said Paul, ignoring her remarks. "Come on."

Melissa had never before travelled farther north than Yorkshire. Paul had fallen asleep as soon as the train had pulled out of the station and so there was no opportunity for any more questions. She made her way to the buffet car and bought herself a gin and tonic and a packet of crisps and returned to her seat. Outside the windows of the train, the bleak February landscape rolled past.

Paul awoke at Newcastle. He stretched and yawned and then blinked at Melissa for a few moments, as if wondering who she was. "Your hair's different," he said suddenly. Melissa stiffened. "It's odd," said Paul, "but I like it. Makes you look like a bird."

"I thought you hadn't even noticed," commented Melissa.

"I nearly didn't recognize you at the station," confessed Paul. "But then I saw your eyes. No one else has eyes like that. They're very fine."

Melissa smiled at Paul affectionately. What man, since the days of Jane Austen, had ever told a girl she had fine eyes? "You'd better tell me who's going," she said. "I thought it was just to be us. But you said something about your mother..."

"Oh, they'll all be there," said Paul, "waiting for the old man to drop off his perch and leave them something. Mother will be there with Jeffrey, my stepfather. He's a stockbroker and a dry old stick. He's Andrew Trent's brother. Then there's old Andrew's adopted son Charles, a layabout, and his fiancée, who rejoices in the name Titchy Gold. His sisters, Angela and Betty, arsenic and old lace, will be there as well."

"And what is Mr. Andrew Trent like?"

"Perfectly horrible. A practical joker of the worst kind. I can't stand him."

"Then why are we going?"

"Mother ordered me to go."

"And do you usually do what your mother orders you to do?"

"Most of the time," said Paul. "Makes life more peaceful."

"Paul, don't you think it's a bit odd of you to ask me to go with you? I mean, it's not as if we've been going out and, I mean..."

"I wanted someone from outside the family with me," said Paul. "Besides, I like you an awful lot."

Melissa smiled at him to hide the fact that she was dreading the meeting with his mother.

"Where do we go after we reach Inverness?" she asked.

"There's no train further north today. I wanted to stay the night in Inverness and travel up in the morning, but Mother said to take a cab. She wanted me to motor up with them, but I don't like Jeffrey much."

"How much will a cab cost?"

"About fifty pounds."

"Gosh, can you afford that?"

"Mother can. And she's paying."

Mother, mother, mother, thought Melissa uneasily. Would there be a shop open in Inverness where she could buy a hair dye?

But the train was late and it was nearly nine o'clock

on a freezing evening when they landed on the platform at Inverness station. There was a taxi waiting
for them at the end of the platform. Jan had ordered it
to pick her son up.

As the cab swept them northwards, it began to
snow, lightly at first and then in great blinding sheets.
"Just as well we decided to get to Arrat House this
evening," said Paul. "We'll probably be snowed in in
the morning."

"Perhaps the others won't make it," suggested
Melissa hopefully.

"I'm sure they will. Jeffrey drives like a fiend.
As far as I could gather, the rest were flying up to
Inverness and going on by cab as well."

Melissa relapsed into an uneasy silence. What
did it matter what Paul's mother thought of her?
She wasn't engaged to him. They hadn't even held
hands.

But her courage deserted her when they drove up
to Arrat House. The house was floodlit and the snow
had thinned a little, so she saw what looked like a
huge mansion, formidable and terrifying.

The taxi driver said blithely he would need to
spend the night in the village. No hope of getting
back to Inverness.

A manservant—*a manservant!* thought Melissa—
came out of the house and took their bags and they
followed him in. The suffocating heat of the house
struck them like a blow. The entrance hall was large

and square. There was a tartan carpet on the floor and antlers and deerskins hung on the wall. Two tartan-covered armchairs, a different tartan from the carpet, stood in front of a blazing log fire.

They followed the manservant up the stairs. He opened a bedroom door and put their bags into it. "You'd better find a separate room for Miss Clarke, Enrico," said Paul.

"I will ask Mr. Trent," said the servant.

"Bit cheeky of him to think we were sleeping together," said Melissa.

"You weren't expected," said Paul patiently. "I haven't been here for ages. He probably thought we were married."

Enrico returned and picked up Melissa's suitcase and asked her to follow him. Her room turned out to be three doors away from Paul's. It was hot but comfortable with a large double bed, a desk and chair at the window, and a low table and chair in front of the fire, but somehow impersonal, like an hotel room. Enrico murmured that she was expected in the drawing-room, which was to the right of the hall. As soon as he had gone, Melissa turned off the radiators and opened the window. A howling blizzard blew in and she quickly closed it again. She found she had a private bathroom. She scrubbed the white make-up from her face and found a plain black wool dress in her suitcase. She had one pair of tights and a pair of plain black court shoes with medium heels. I look like a French tart, she thought in despair, but went along to Paul's room, only to find he was not there.

Fighting back a feeling of dread, she went down to the drawing-room.

All eyes turned to meet her. The room was covered in tartan carpet of a noisy yellow and red. The sofa and chairs were upholstered in pink brocade and the lamps about the room had pink pleated silk shades.

Her host, Mr. Andrew Trent, was standing in front of the fire, leaning on a stick. He looked remarkably healthy. He had thick grey hair and a wizened, wrinkled face, small eyes, large nose, and a fleshy mouth. He looked like an elderly comedian of the old school, the kind who pinched bums and told blue jokes. He was wearing a black velvet jacket, a lace shirt, tartan waistcoat and kilt, which revealed thin old shanks covered in tartan stockings.

Paul came forward and introduced Melissa. Melissa murmured good evening to all and found a chair in a corner. She was hungry and there were plates of sandwiches on a low table in front of the fire, but she did not dare move to get one. Which was Paul's mother?

Titchy Gold was immediately recognizable, and the incredibly good-looking young man at her side must be Charles. The two frumps must be the arsenic-and-old-lace sisters. That left a dry stick of a man and a thin elegant woman who was glaring at Melissa as if she could not believe her eyes. She could be none other than Paul's mother.

Melissa cowered in her corner. Why didn't Paul join her?

Melissa had belonged to off-beat left-wing groups when at university and adopted their style of dress, not out of any political commitment but out of a working-class inferiority complex. She was actually painfully shy and tried to cover up her shyness with noisy clothes and an occasionally abrupt manner. Somehow, for a brief period, neither clothes nor shyness had troubled her at the research centre. She was too absorbed in her work. It was a strange job for someone who had previously marched in antinuclear protests, but she had secured an excellent physics degree and had been offered a well-paying job at the research centre and had taken it without a qualm of conscience.

A woman of Spanish appearance dressed in black entered the room. She picked up the plates of sandwiches and began to hand them round, eventually approaching Melissa's corner. Melissa gratefully took three. The woman asked her if she would like a glass of wine and Melissa murmured that she would.

She was just biting into her first sandwich when Jan came and stood over her. "Paul hadn't told us about you," said Jan.

Melissa waited.

"I mean, it was a bit rude to spring you on us. He might have warned us." Jan stood with one hip jutting out, one skeletal beringed hand resting on it. Her eyes were slightly protuberant, the sort of eyes usually found in a fatter face. Her mouth was very thin and painted scarlet. "How long have you known my son?"

"I have been working at the research centre for some months now," said Melissa. "Paul is a colleague, that's all. He asked me to join him on this visit."

"And of course you jumped at it," said Jan, contemptuously. "Do you always wear your hair like that?"

"Are you always so rude?" countered Melissa.

"Don't be cheeky," said Jan. "I can tell by that accent of yours, Surrey with the whinge on top, that you are not used to this sort of society. Nor will you become so, if I have anything to say about it."

"Piss off," said Melissa furiously.

Jan gave a mocking laugh and returned to her son. She said something to him and he shrugged and then crossed the room and sat down next to Melissa. "Your mother doesn't think I'm good enough for you," said Melissa.

"Don't let it bother you. She wouldn't consider anyone good enough."

Melissa was twenty-three, an age she had hitherto felt classified her as a mature woman. Now she felt quite weepy and childlike. She thought of her parents, Mum and Dad in the shabby terraced house in Reading with its poky rooms and weedy garden. She had her own flat now, but as soon as she got out of this hell-hole, she would go and see them. Never again would she be ashamed of her background.

There was love and warmth there and comfort. Sod Paul for having dragged her into this!

But her mood was soon to lighten. Jan was complaining about the heat from the fire. "Sit over here, Jan," urged old Andrew Trent, his eyes twinkling. He indicated an armchair a good bit away from the fire. Jan sank down gracefully into it and then there came the sound of a large long-drawn-out fart. Jan flew up, her face scarlet. "It's one of those damned cushions," she started to rage, but then, mindful of the reason for the visit, she forced a smile on her face. "What a joker you are, Andrew," she said, and the old man cackled with glee.

"I think Mr. Trent's rather an old duck," said Melissa.

"Don't say that," said Paul. "Wait till he really gets started. He isn't ill at all, you see. He must have been feeling lonely. Now he's got a whole houseful of people to torment."

"Can't we just leave . . . in the morning?"

"It's snowing a blizzard. Enrico says we'll be trapped for days."

Melissa looked across the room. Mr. Trent was watching her. He dropped one eyelid in a wink. Melissa smiled. She thought he was sweet.

The party broke up at eleven o'clock and they all went off to their respective rooms. Paul accompanied

Melissa to her door. He stood for a moment moving from foot to foot and staring at her. Then he seized her hand and shook it. "Good night," he said and scurried off to his own room.

Melissa shrugged and pushed open her door, noticing as she did so that it was already a little ajar. A bag of flour, which had been balanced over the door and was intended to burst over her, fell instead in one piece, striking her a stunning blow. She clutched her head and reeled forward and sank to her knees on the carpet. "Ha! Ha! Ha! He! He! He! Haw! Haw! Haw!" cackled a voice. Still holding her head, she stumbled to her feet, looking around wildly as the hideous cackling went on and on. She found a joke machine, which was producing the hellish laughter, had been hidden behind the clock on the mantelpiece. She seized it and shook it but it went on laughing, so she wrenched open the window and threw the thing out into the white raging blizzard.

Paul Sinclair had been prepared for jokes, but came to the conclusion that he was to be left alone and began to relax. He opened his shirt drawer to take out a clean shirt for the morning and two clockwork paper bats flew up into his face. Nonetheless, he felt he had got off lightly.

Angela Trent found her father had sewn up the bottoms of her pyjamas. Betty, who was sharing a room with her sister, lay in bed giggling as Angela swore terrible oaths as she looked for her sewing scissors to cut the bottoms of the pyjama legs open. But as Betty lay laughing, she clutched her favourite hot-water bottle in the shape of a teddy bear to her bosom. It began to leak all over her and her laughter changed to squawks of outrage and dismay. Her father had punctured her hot-water bottle.

Charles lay stretched out on the top of the bed and watched Titchy Gold as, clad only in a brief nightie, she went to see if the housekeeper had hung away her clothes properly. Charles and Titchy were not sharing a bedroom, but Charles planned to enjoy a little lovemaking before retiring to his own room. Titchy opened the carved door of a massive Victorian wardrobe and a body with a knife thrust in its chest fell down on top of her. She screamed and screamed hysterically. The bedroom door opened and Andrew Trent stood there, leaning on his stick and laughing until the tears ran down his face. Behind him gathered the other guests.

"It's a joke, Titchy. A dummy," said Charles, taking the hysterical girl in his arms. "Come to bed. It's too bad of you, Dad. Your jokes are over the top." When Mr. Trent and his guests went away, Titchy howled that she was leaving in the morning.

Charles soothed her down. "Look, I've been thinking, Titchy. Dad's an old man. He's enjoying himself and, yes, he tricked us all into coming here by saying he was at death's door. Why don't we just charm the old money-bags and pretend his jokes are funny? He can't live forever. If he drops off, then I inherit, and we'll have loads of money."

"Are you sure?" Titchy dried her eyes and gazed up at him.

"Sure as sure. He's Trent Baby Foods, isn't he? Worth millions. Come to bed."

The fastidious Jeffrey Trent removed his contact lenses and said to his wife, "Well, at least he has had the decency not to play any tricks on me. But dying he most certainly is not. I will get out of here as soon as possible if I have to charter a helicopter to do so."

His wife held up the phone receiver of the extension in their room. "Dead," she said. "We're cut off."

"Tcha!" said Jeffrey. He went into their bathroom to urinate before going to bed.

But he did not notice until it was too late that the practical joker had covered the top of the toilet with thin adhesive transparent plastic.

Melissa slept heavily and awoke to the sound of a gong beating on the air. The door opened and Paul walked in. "Aren't you dressed yet?" he exclaimed. "We're all expected at the breakfast table at nine. House rules."

"I haven't telepathic powers," groaned Melissa. "Why didn't you tell me last night? God, I feel sick. That old bastard put a bag of flour over the door and it hit me a stunning blow on the head. He should be certified. Did anything happen to you? And poor Titchy."

"I got clockwork bats in the shirt drawer. I'll see you downstairs."

"No, you don't!" Melissa scrambled out of bed. "I'm not facing that lot on my own. What's the weather like?"

Paul pulled aside the curtains. Together they looked out at the bleak whiteness of driving snow. "Damn!" muttered Melissa. "Trapped. Wait here, Paul. I won't be a minute."

She grabbed some clothes and went into the bathroom. She stripped off her transparent pink nightie—Paul hadn't even noticed it—and pulled on her underwear and an old pair of jeans and a "Ban the Bomb" sweater.

"I wouldn't wear that," said Paul firmly. "Not the sweater. We're working on nuclear power, remember?"

"But not bombs. Wait! I'll put on a blouse instead. This place is too hot for a sweater anyway." She stripped off the sweater. Would Paul notice the fetching lacy bra? No, Paul was staring in an unseeing way out of the window. She put on a man's white shirt and tied the ends at her waist.

The dining-room was in an uproar when they entered. Betty was sitting with yellow egg yolk streaming down her face. Charles and Titchy were laughing in a forced way. Andrew Trent was laughing so hard he looked as if he might have a seizure, and Jeffrey,

Jan and Angela were in states of suppressed rage. It transpired that the old practical joker had put a device under the tablecloth and under Betty's breakfast. He had then pressed a connecting lever and some wire spring had hurled the contents of Betty's plate straight into her face.

"You old fool," growled Angela. "One day someone will throttle the life out of you and it might be me."

"Did you cut the phones off?" demanded Jeffrey.

"Not I," said his brother, wiping his streaming eyes with his napkin. "Snow's brought the lines down."

Enrico's wife, who, it transpired, was called Maria, quietly came in with a basin of water and a face towel, which she presented to Betty before taking her ruined breakfast away. Enrico then came in with another plate of bacon and eggs. The Spanish servants glided noiselessly to and fro as if nothing out of the way had happened. What brought them to the far north of Scotland, to bleak Sutherland? wondered Melissa. Possibly the pay was good.

Jan made an effort to be polite to Melissa, as did everyone else. But then, they were drawing together against the menace that was Andrew Trent. Melissa wondered how they were all going to pass the time, but there was an extensive library, a conservatory, and a games room in the basement, with billiards and a table tennis. She joined Paul in the library, where they read until lunch. Lunch was a quiet affair.

Andrew Trent seemed abstracted. In the afternoon the old man went up to bed. Melissa and Paul and Titchy and Charles played a noisy game of table tennis. Melissa began to think she might enjoy her stay after all.

After dinner, instead of retiring to the drawing-room, they were invited to assemble in the hall. The fire was burning low and the hall was lit by candlelight. Extra chairs had been brought in and they all sat in a circle round the fire.

"How old is this house?" asked Melissa. "I mean, it's all been modernized with central heating and that, but the walls look old."

"Oh, it's very old," said Mr. Trent. He leaned forward in his chair, his hands folded on the handle of his stick and his chin resting on them. "About the fourteenth century. As a matter of fact, it's haunted."

"Rubbish, Andrew," said Jeffrey.

"I believe in ghosts," said Titchy suddenly.

"There's one here, all right," said Mr. Trent. "It's the ghost of an English knight."

"Tell us," squealed Titchy, clapping her hands.

"Yes, do tell us what an English knight was doing in Scotland in the fourteenth century," sneered Jeffrey.

"His name was Sir Guy Montfour," said Mr. Trent dreamily. "He had returned from a crusade. On his way back through France he met Mary Mackay, the daughter of the chieftain of the Clan Mackay. He fell in love with her. But the Mackays left during the night. He decided to pursue them to Scotland"—his voice sank eerily—"to this very house."

"I don't believe a word of this," muttered Paul, but Melissa felt the spell the old man was casting on the group. The candles flickered in a slight draught and a log shifted in the hearth.

"The chieftain pretended to welcome Sir Guy. Mary was obviously in love with the knight. The very next day, Mary was seized by the clan servants and taken to the coast. She was put on a boat to Norway, where she spent the rest of her life in exile. But Sir Guy...ah...what a tragedy!"

The wind suddenly moaned around the house. Titchy searched for Charles's hand and gripped it tightly.

"They took Sir Guy out on a stag hunt. He did not know that his Mary had gone. He shot a fine stag up on the mountain. When he was bending over the dead beast, the chieftain took his claymore and sliced the poor knight's head from his body. They buried him on the mountain in an unmarked grave. But he comes back to this house. You can hear the sound of mailed feet in the passage above and then he descends the stairs."

There was another great moaning of the wind... and then they all heard it, a heavy tread and the clink of armour.

"Behold!" cried Mr. Trent suddenly. "Oh, God, he comes!"

The staircase was bathed in a greenish light. And down the stairs clanked a knight in black armour carrying his head under his arm.

Titchy screamed and screamed.

There was a sudden explosion and a great cloud of red smoke billowed about the room. Jeffrey was shouting, "It's a trick!" Titchy was still screaming and screaming. She had leaped up and was drumming her feet on the floor in a sort of ecstasy of panic.

Paul rushed and opened the door and a great gale of wind blew into the hall, clearing the smoke. The knight had disappeared.

Everyone was shouting and exclaiming. Titchy had relapsed into sobs. Old Mr. Trent was clapping his hands and laughing like mad. "You should see your faces," he shouted when he could.

White-faced, Titchy stumbled from the room. She felt terribly ill. She just made it to her bathroom, bent over the toilet and was dreadfully sick.

But the toilet had been sealed with transparent plastic.

Titchy collapsed in a sobbing heap on the bathroom floor, gasping between sobs, "I'll kill him. I'll kill him!"

Chapter Two

A difference of taste in jokes is a
great strain on the affections.

—George Eliot

What added to the tension in Arrat House in the next few days was not only that they were snow-bound or the practical jokes, but the fact that the relatives had decided to pretend to be amused by them. Charles had started it by laughing every time Mr. Trent laughed and that had set up a spirit of competition in the others.

And what an infinite capacity for practical jokes old Mr. Trent seemed to have, from gorse bushes at the bottom of the bed to buckets of freezing water above the door. Cushions made rude noises, machines in corners emitted bursts of maniacal laughter. Melissa became used to holding down her plate of food firmly with her fork to make sure its contents didn't fly up in her face. Melissa, like Paul, felt under no obligation to appear to be amused by Mr. Trent's merry japes and pranks but she did begin to feel as if she were incarcerated in a centrally heated loony-bin.

The snow had stopped, but Enrico remarked that all surrounding roads were blocked. "You will soon run out of food," said Melissa, but Enrico shrugged and said he was always prepared for weather such as this and had plenty of stocks.

Melissa tried to sympathize with the servant, saying it must be a difficult job. Enrico merely froze her with a look and said he considered himself fortunate. He had a slight air of hauteur and carefully accented English. Melissa suspected that, like quite a number of Spaniards, Enrico considered himself a cut above the British and therefore tolerated the foibles of his employer as evidence of a more barbarous race. His small dark wife was even haughtier and more uncommunicative.

As far as Paul was concerned, Melissa wondered why he had invited her. He had not made a pass at her. He seemed to spend an awful lot of time in the library reading. Melissa put on her leather jacket and a pair of combat boots and ventured outside. Enrico had managed to clear some of the snow from the courtyard. The sky above was a bleak grey. The house, seen clearly from the outside, was a large square grey building with turrets on each corner in the French manner, rather like a miniature château. Arrat House lay at the foot of a mountain that reared its menacing bulk up to the sky. The house itself was on a rise, and below, on the right, she could make out the huddled houses of a village.

She peered up at the top of the house. There was no television aerial. Television would have whiled away some of the time, she thought dismally.

She shivered with cold and went back into the house, kicking the door open first with her boot and jumping back in case anything fell from the top of it.

Paul was in the library. She sat down on a chair opposite him and said, "Is there no way we can get out of here?"

He sighed impatiently and marked his place in the book with his finger. "I'm just settling down," said Paul. "We can't do anything else at the moment. Look, do you mind? This book's very interesting."

"Having brought me to this insane asylum, I think you might at least have some concern for my well-being," said Melissa stiffly.

"What else can I do?" he asked edgily. "I mean, it's hardly prison. The food's good. As Mother said—"

"I am not interested in anything your mother says," snapped Melissa, suddenly furious. "I mean, you're all poncing around as if you're lords of the manor, and just look at this dump. It's in the worst of taste. Ghastly tartan carpets and pink lamps. Yuk!"

"I would have thought," said Paul in a thin voice,

"that any female sporting pink hair and combat boots did not know the meaning of taste. Mother said..."

Melissa stood up. She told Paul and his mother to go and perform impossible anatomical acts on themselves and stormed out.

She went up to her room and sat on the end of the bed and stared bleakly about her. She had a longing for her mother, to put her head down on that aproned bosom which always seemed to smell of onions and cry her eyes out.

The door opened and Paul walked in. "What do you want?" demanded Melissa.

He sat down on the end of the bed next to her and blinked at her owlishly. "I just wanted to say I liked your hair," he said, taking her hand. "You've washed all that gel out of it and now it looks like pink feathers."

"Did your mother give you permission to say that?"

"Come off it, Melissa. I'm a bit on edge. This is all wrong, you know. I'd been working up courage to ask you out since I first saw you. It was your eyes, I think, so large and grey. We should have gone out for dinner and... and talked, but here we are. I don't really want to talk about Mother. Except to point out that it's easier to love than to be loved. She is very possessive. My father was a quiet, unambitious man. I think she divorced him to marry Jeffrey because she wanted nothing but the best for me—best school, best university. I...I'm glad I'm free in a way now, and that I've got my own place and work I like. You wouldn't know anything about that. I mean, about being shy and burying yourself in your work. You've probably got lots of friends."

"Not really," said Melissa. With a burst of rare candour, she added, "I'm a terrible snob, really. I'm so ashamed of my working-class background that I adopt poses. I'm shy, too. I wasn't even a good left-winger. I'm not really interested in any politics. I just went along with it at university because it gave me a role to play. So when I joined the atomic research centre, I dropped all my old acquaintances. They were very excited at first about me having the job and saying I could give them inside information and I got frightened and didn't see them again. So we're very alike in a way."

He carefully removed his glasses and put them in his pocket. He took her by the shoulders and deposited a clumsy kiss on her lips. Melissa wrapped her arms around him and kissed him back.

"Wow," he said shakily. He turned brick-red and fumbled in his pocket for his glasses and put them on. He walked to the window and looked out, and then he gave an exclamation. "Come here! Look at this!"

Melissa joined him. Down below, Enrico was making his way out of the courtyard on skis.

"Can you ski?" asked Paul.

"Yes, as a matter of fact, I can."

"Ever done any cross-country skiing?"

"Yes, I went on holiday once to a ski resort in the French Alps, one of these cheap student trips."

Paul's eyes blazed with excitement. "We could ask Enrico if he's got another pair and if we can borrow them. Then we'll pack up what we need. There's a couple of old rucksacks in a cupboard in the game room. We'll just take off. I'll get a map. We could even go across country to Inverness if we start very early in the morning and the weather stays clear. What do you say?"

"You mean, get out of here? I'd love it."

"We won't tell anyone. We'll just send the skis back when we get to Inverness with the British Rail door-to-door delivery service. Everyone will think we're going off for a day's skiing. Let them all stay here and suck up to the old man if they want!"

"As soon as the roads clear, we must get out of here," said Angela Trent to her sister.

"Is that wise?" asked Betty. "I mean, Dad can be very quirky. He pays us an annual allowance, but he could stop that any time he felt like it—and worse. He could leave us nothing in his will. We've never worked at anything. We're too old to start now."

There was a light *ping* from the phone extension. Angela picked it up. "It's working again," she said.

"That's something anyway. I don't think I can stand much more of this, Betty."

"Well, I don't like it," snapped Betty, "but there is no way I am leaving the field clear for the others. Have you noticed how Charles and that Titchy girl are playing up to Dad?"

"Yes," said Angela with a frown. "Something's got to be done about that pair. Dad's stopped playing tricks on Titchy and she's making goo-goo eyes at him and he's loving it."

"I'll think of something," said Betty. "You're all talk and no *do*, Angela."

"And you're all bitch, bitch, bitch."

The sisters fell to squabbling, although Angela was half-hearted about it. She was thinking about Titchy.

When Betty pointed out that Angela was badly in need of a shave, Angela used that as an excuse to storm out. She went quietly along the corridor and opened the door to Titchy's room, in the same way as everyone else at Arrat House had quickly learned to open doors—standing well back for a few moments after she did so. The room was empty.

She walked in and shut the door behind her. She opened the wardrobe and stood looking at Titchy's array of gorgeous dresses, dresses which Titchy had paid a fortune for, knowing that her fortune lay more in how she looked than in any acting ability.

They all looked like tart's clothes to Angela, so she

studied the labels and finally selected five that bore the name of a famous couture house. She extracted a razor blade from her pocket that she had taken from her toilet-bag while rowing with Betty and got to work.

Titchy went up to dress for dinner. She liked making an appearance. She took out a low-cut scarlet silk chiffon dinner gown and laid it on the bed. After a bath and change of underwear, she wriggled into the gown. All her couture models were taken to a dressmaker and then fitted tightly onto her body. With a faint sigh, the dress fell from her and lay on the floor.

With trembling hands she picked it up. The seams had been neatly sliced. Only a few threads had been left to hold it together.

Hate for old Mr. Trent boiled up in her. She had played up to him to please Charles. She had made eyes at the old fright and had only giggled when he had felt her bottom.

She searched frantically through her other dresses. Four had been similarly treated.

They were all gathered in the drawing-room before dinner when Titchy marched in, an armful of dresses over her arm. She flung them down in front of Mr. Trent and screamed, "You miserable old fart. That's hundreds of pounds of my best clothes you've ruined, you senile old fruit."

In all her amazement, Melissa nonetheless noted

that Titchy had dropped her breathy Marilyn Monroe act and looked as hard as steel. Mr. Trent's startled cry of "I had nothing to do with it" went ignored by the angry actress.

"I don't know how I'm going to get out of here, but I'm going to manage it somehow," raged Titchy. "I'll send you the bill when I get to London. Who the hell do you all think you are anyway? Parasites, that's what you are. But I work for my money. 'Be nice to the old man,' says Charles, so I have to put up with insane jokes and your dirty old man's hands fumbling at me. You can keep your money-bags. Stuff the lot of you!"

There was a deathly silence when she left. Then Paul began to laugh. "Don't you see how *right* she is?" he cried.

"Paul!" said Jan furiously. "Remember where you are."

She looked uneasily at Mr. Trent. He had sat impassive during Titchy's tirade. Now he looked slowly around the room, his old eyes glittering in a reptilian way. Melissa shuddered. Tomorrow she and Paul would be far away. Hang on to that thought.

To their surprise, Titchy appeared at the dinner table, icily calm. It was a silent meal. Mr. Trent sat brooding at the head of the table, his eyes occasionally travelling from one face to the other.

They filed back to the drawing-room afterwards. Everyone longed to escape from the heavy atmosphere but it was as if the power of the old man's personality was keeping them prisoner.

Then Charles whispered to Titchy, "Come outside. We need to talk."

"Very well," said Titchy. "But it won't do you any good."

Wrapped up warmly, she and Charles went outside into the courtyard. It was a bright night with a hard frost.

"Titchy," pleaded Charles, "don't go. There's no way you can leave yet."

"I don't care," said Titchy. "I don't care if I only get as far as the village. I'll find a room there. I'm not staying with that madman."

"Titchy, I do love you. We're going to be married."

"And live on what?" demanded Titchy. "Look, Charles, that old fruitcake could live forever. I'm not a fool. I can't act for peanuts, and after my looks go, I'll get a few television quiz shows and then that'll be that. I don't want to end up married to a man I have to keep supporting."

"But I have a job!"

"Selling vitamin pills? When did you last sell any? You're just about to drop that job like you dropped the others. It's no good, Charles. I've had it."

Charles's usual sunny optimism deserted him. "I hate that old bastard," he muttered. "Why doesn't he die? God, I'd like to stick a knife in his guts."

"Come off it," said Titchy wearily. "Start thinking

seriously about making some money yourself. Thank God, I haven't any rich relatives. You've no idea how sick you all seem, hovering around that dreadful man waiting for him to pop off."

Upstairs, Melissa began to pack as much of her belongings as she could into the rucksack Paul had given her. At one point she looked out of the window. The two figures were still there below, Titchy and Charles, pacing up and down, arguing.

The door opened and Jan walked in. Melissa swung round and stared at her defiantly.

"Just a little chat, dear," cooed Jan. "As one woman to another, I must appeal to you to do something about Paul."

"I don't think anything needs to be done," said Melissa.

"But surely you must see he is jeopardizing his future. Charles is a hopeless case. Andrew Trent must see that Paul is the finer person. Although Andrew has appointed a managing director to run his factories, someone has to take over when he dies."

Melissa was horrified. "Paul is a very good scientist. You would not like to see him waste his education by selling baby food."

"Running a multi-million operation is not selling baby food," said Jan acidly.

"It's no use coming to me," retorted Melissa firmly. "My advice to Paul would be to have nothing to do with the Trent fortune."

Jan's face hardened. "I should have known better than to try to talk sense to a common little slut like you."

"You'd better leave before I slap you," said Melissa in a voice which to her fury she realized was trembling.

Jan got up. "What a nightmare this is," she said half to herself. "The old fool shows no signs of dying. I could kill him myself and not suffer one qualm of conscience. Oh, why am I wasting time with a Communist prig?"

She went out and slammed the door behind her.

Melissa sat down abruptly, feeling sick and shaken.

"Did *you* cut up Titchy's dresses?" Betty was asking.

"I didn't cut them up," said Angela gruffly. "Just opened up the seams. She can stitch them up easily enough with a needle and thread."

"W-e-l-l-l," breathed Betty in reluctant admiration. "I wouldn't have guessed you'd have had the backbone. All that mannish talk of yours is usually empty bluster, sister dear."

"You nasty ferret," said Angela. "I'm going down for a nightcap. All you can do in life is back-seat drive, Betty. It's all you've ever done. Point out everyone else's faults but never look at your own. If anyone in this house had any guts, they'd put dear Dad out of our misery for once and for all."

"Words, words, words," jeered Betty.

*   *   *

Titchy joined the others over the drinks tray in the drawing-room to warm up a bit after her talk with Charles. Everyone kept saying good night and then coming back in. Jan approached Mr. Trent and whispered to him. Then her place was taken by Jeffrey, who had a low-voiced conversation with his brother. Then Angela. Then Betty. Charles watched them all. Mr. Trent rose to his feet and hobbled to the door. Charles made a half-move towards him, then shrugged and helped himself to another drink. Angela and Betty said good night and went out together. Jan and Jeffrey followed them. Then, ten minutes later, Angela returned, saying moodily she would like to wring Betty's neck, and sat down by the fire. Melissa had finished her packing and joined Paul, who was drinking whisky. He said something to her and shot out of the room, to return some fifteen minutes later. It's like a French farce, thought Melissa, people coming and going.

At last she decided she had better get some sleep. She went up to her room and carefully felt the end of the bed. There was a lump. She put her hand under the covers and drew out a stuffed hedgehog, and with an exclamation of disgust she opened the window and threw it out into the snow. She set her alarm for six o'clock—she had agreed to meet Paul downstairs at six-thirty—and then got ready for bed.

Titchy, too, went to her room. She was feeling much better. She had discovered her dresses only needed restitching. It was a pity about Charles. He was the nicest, handsomest man she knew, but there was no future in marrying him.

She went to the large Victorian wardrobe to get out her clothes and pack them ready for her escape in the morning. As she swung open the door, a body wearing a monster mask and with a large knife stuck in its chest fell towards her. Trembling, she leaped back and then she stared down at the horror in disgust. Frightful Mr. Trent had played his last trick on her. After tomorrow, she would never see Charles or any of his dreadful relatives again. She stepped over the figure and took her clothes down from their hangers and then carried them to the bed and packed them all neatly in one large suitcase. She had a leisurely bath and then climbed into bed.

Half an hour later, Charles opened the door of her room. A pink-shaded lamp was burning beside the bed. Titchy was lying asleep, her fluffy blonde curls shining in the lamplight. Intent on his purpose, he did not appear to notice the dark figure on the floor beside the wardrobe, for it was lying outside the pool of light cast by the little lamp.

He took off his dressing-gown and crept into bed beside Titchy and took her in his arms. She murmured a sleepy protest. He began to make love to her feverishly until she responded, finally feeling he had excelled himself. He tried to get her to promise she would now stay, but Titchy said evasively, "We'll see."

He went off to his own room feeling happier.

*   *   *

Melissa awoke with her alarm and quickly got ready and then went downstairs. Paul was already waiting for her with the skis and boots. Giggling with excitement, they strapped on their boots and carried the skis outside where they put them on.

It was still dark but a clear moon was shining down on the glittering landscape. They pushed their way forward until they were on top of the rise leading down into the village.

"Race you!" shouted Paul, and off they both went, the skis hissing over the snow, the clear air streaming past them, and the shadow of Arrat House falling away behind them.

Melissa had never known such exhilaration, such freedom. Paul was waiting for her when she came to a stop in the middle of the village.

"You know," panted Melissa. "I've just realized it. Mr. Trent *frightened* me."

Paul looked at her solemnly. "Yes," he said slowly. "There was an awful atmosphere in that house. Well, we're away now and we're not going back. Not ever!"

When Titchy awoke, the sun was blazing into the room. She stretched languorously. Then she sat up in bed and yawned and rubbed her eyes. She glanced distastefully at the crumpled figure on the floor and then went very still. There was something very...

well...human about that body. And...and...the
blood which had seeped and was staining the dummy's white shirt-front looked very real and not at
all like stage blood, or Kensington Gore, as it was
called.

"Nothing but a trick. Nothing but a trick," she said
as she edged out of bed. She stooped down over the
dummy and reached behind and untied the strings
that held the ridiculous monster mask in place.

The dead face of old Andrew Trent looked up
at her.

Although Police Constable Hamish Macbeth had
Sergeant MacGregor's area around Cnothan as well
as his own to cover, the sergeant being away on holiday, he had been undisturbed by crime of any kind.
The village of Lochdubh seemed asleep under its
blanket of thick snow.

January had been an unusually mild month but
February had turned out miserably cold. Hamish lit
the stove in the kitchen and wondered, not for the
first time, whether he could persuade headquarters at
Strathbane to put in central heating.

And then the phone through in the office began
to ring. He expected it was a friend. He hoped it was
Priscilla Halburton-Smythe, a particular friend. He
had not seen her for some weeks and had begun to
wonder why she was keeping away from him.

"Lochdubh police," said Hamish in his gentle Highland accent.

"Murder!" screamed the voice.

"Now then," said Hamish quickly. "Easy now. What murder? Who's been murdered?"

"Andrew Trent at Arrat House."

"Indeed!" said Hamish coldly. Once Mr. Trent himself had phoned and said there was a dead body in his library. Sergeant MacGregor had been away then as well, so Hamish had gone himself, the village of Arrat being part of MacGregor's beat. There was indeed a body in the library, covered in blood. He was just bending over it when the body had jumped up and had given him the shock of his life. It was the manservant, Enrico, covered in fake blood.

"Are you sure it iss not a practical joke?" asked Hamish, whose voice always became more sibilant when he was upset or excited.

"No, you fool. This is Mr. Trent's daughter Angela. I'm telling you, someone has stuck a knife in him."

"I'll be over there as quick as I can. What are the roads like?"

"Good God, man," squawked Angela's voice. "How the hell should I know? Still blocked, I suppose. Use a helicopter or something."

Hamish rang off. He picked up the phone again to call the headquarters in Strathbane, but then he slowly replaced the receiver. He had done that after the call about the body in the library and had been made to look a fool when the heavyweights from Strathbane and a whole forensic team had arrived. He put on his uniform and placed his skis and boots in the back of the police Land Rover.

This time he would make sure it really was a murder.

Chapter Three

A joke's a very serious thing.

—Charles Churchill

Hamish did not have to use his skis. The snow-ploughs had been out in force. He found himself hoping desperately, as he drove slowly along narrow roads banked by snow-drifts, that it really was another of old Mr. Trent's practical jokes.

He was met at the door of Arrat House by Enrico, who inclined his head in the best English butler manner and asked if the constable would like to view the body.

"Good Heffens, man, that's what I'm here for," said Hamish testily, and then felt himself begin to relax. It was surely all a joke.

He still thought it was a joke when he was led down to the games room. Mr. Trent was neatly laid out on the billiard table, with tall candles burning on either side of his head. His hands holding a crucifix were folded on his breast.

Maria, Enrico's wife, was kneeling on the floor, a rosary slipping between her fingers, mumbling prayers.

Hamish approached the body gingerly, quite prepared for Mr. Trent to leap up cackling with laughter. But that face was so very dead. Hamish bent down and listened to Mr. Trent's chest. Then he rose slowly, his face a picture of outrage.

"He iss dead!"

"Yes," said Enrico. "Of course he is dead. Brutal murder."

"How was he killed?"

"He was stabbed with a knife...here." Enrico pointed to the dead man's chest. Hamish looked down at the pristine white of the shirt-front.

"Where was he murdered?"

"Upstairs. In the wardrobe in Miss Gold's bedroom."

"Good God, man. *You moved the body!*"

"It was only fitting."

"And you changed his clothes?"

"Of course. His shirt was covered in blood."

"You are an idiot," exclaimed Hamish, horrified. "This is murder. You should have left everything untouched. Who is in this house? Miss Angela Trent made the telephone call."

"There is Mr. Jeffrey Trent, and his wife; Miss

Angela and Miss Betty; the adopted son, Charles; his lady friend, Titchy Gold; and Mrs. Jeffrey's son, Paul Sinclair; and *his* lady friend, Miss Clarke."

Hamish walked to a phone extension in the corner of the room. He phoned police headquarters in Strathbane and reported the murder, telling an outraged Detective Chief Inspector Blair that the body had been moved and laid out in the games room by the servants.

Then he grimly asked to be taken first to see Mr. Jeffrey Trent.

But the door opened and Jeffrey walked in. He gave a wincing look at the body.

Hamish introduced himself and then said severely, "Surely you, sir, could have stopped this? Nothing should have been touched."

"They did it without asking me," said Jeffrey plaintively. He held up a plastic bag. "I've got the knife here that was taken out of his chest."

Hamish took it from him and studied it. The haft was of painted wood and belonged to one of those trick knives where the dummy blade slides up into the haft. But this one had had a thin sharp steel blade substituted. It was still smeared with blood.

"You'd better show me where he was killed," said Hamish. "Who found the body?"

"Titchy Gold."

Hamish turned to Enrico, "Get her and bring her along."

Jeffrey led the way upstairs to Titchy's bedroom. Hamish stood in the doorway and looked into the room. The bed was made up, the wardrobe door closed, and the air smelled of some sort of cleaner.

He turned in amazement to Enrico, who had returned quietly after summoning Titchy. "Don't tell me, just don't tell me, that you've cleaned this room."

"Maria did it," said Enrico. "There was blood on the carpet. She could not leave a mess like that."

"You," said Hamish, "are in bad trouble, and if the chief inspector does not charge you with interfering in a murder investigation, you can count yourself lucky."

Enrico looked unmoved. "Here's Titchy," said Jeffrey.

Titchy Gold and Hamish Macbeth surveyed each other. Titchy threw him a tremulous smile, thinking he was quite nice-looking with those hazel eyes and that fiery red hair.

Hamish thought Titchy looked as if she had stepped down from one of the calendars usually hung in motor repair shops. She was wearing a brief tight scarlet leather skirt with a transparent white blouse, seamed stockings and very high-heeled red shoes. Her dyed blonde hair was piled on top of her head, apart from a few artistic wisps. Her face was beautifully made up with a small lascivious mouth painted pink and false eyelashes shading bright blue eyes.

"Miss Gold, before I take your official statement, just tell me briefly what happened."

Titchy shuddered. "I found the body when I opened the wardrobe last night. It just fell out. He— Mr. Trent—had played a joke on me before where a dummy with a knife in it fell out of that wardrobe. I was fed up. I was getting out of here somehow. So I just left the body lying where it was and went to bed. It was when I awoke in the morning that I thought there was something funny about it and...and...I took off the mask...and..."

She dabbed at her eyes. Hamish looked at her narrowly. He sensed that Titchy was excited about something rather than shocked or frightened.

"I'm going to lock this room," said Hamish to Jeffrey, "in the hope that there's something left for forensic to examine. While we wait for the team to arrive from Strathbane, I may as well take preliminary statements. Is there a room I can use?"

"The library," offered Jeffrey. "It's got a desk."

"Very well. Lead the way."

As they were going down the stairs, a thin elegant woman darted up to Jeffrey and seized him by the arm. "It's Paul," she cried, waving a letter. "He's gone off with that girl. What are we..." Her voice trailed away as she saw Hamish.

"Your son Paul Sinclair and Miss Clarke have left," said Hamish. "What does he say in that letter? You are Mrs. Jeffrey Trent, I gather."

Jan clutched the letter to her bosom.

"It's private," she gasped. "Private correspondence."

Hamish held out his hand. "Nothing is private in a murder investigation, Mrs. Trent. Hand it over."

Jan looked wildly at her husband, who shrugged. Reluctantly she gave the letter to Hamish. It said:

Dear Mum,

We can't stand the old man's jokes any longer so we're getting out. If I had stayed a day longer, I would have killed the silly old fool. I'll call on you in London when I get back. Tell Enrico we're sending the skis back from Inverness.

Love, Paul

Hamish put the letter in his pocket. "Now for the library," he said. "First I've got to make a phone call. Mr. Trent, give me a description of Mr. Sinclair and Miss Clarke."

"No," wailed Jan.

"He'll need to be brought back," said Jeffrey quietly. "Don't make things worse." He turned to Hamish. "Paul is about six feet tall, fair hair, horn-rimmed glasses, twenty-five. I don't know what he's wearing, but probably something suitable for skiing. Melissa Clarke is about a couple of years younger, five feet, six inches, pink hair, protest student-demo clothes."

"Right!" Hamish picked up the phone and got through to the Inverness police and gave them a description of Paul and Melissa, saying that they might be found at the rail station waiting for a train south.

"Now," said Hamish, sitting behind the desk which was placed at the window. "I'll start with you, Mr. Trent. Mrs. Trent, I will see you later." Jan looked as if she would have liked to protest, but Jeffrey pointedly held the door open for her.

"It's a bad business," sighed Jeffrey. "It can't be any of us. Probably some maniac got in from outside."

Hamish studied Jeffrey for a long moment. Jeffrey was a grey man—grey hair, grey suit, greyish complexion. He showed no signs of grief.

"First of all," said Hamish, "why are you all gathered here at this time of year? I mean, it's not Christmas or Easter or the summer holidays."

"Andrew wrote to us all and said he was dying," said Jeffrey in a dry precise voice. "We should have known it was a lie. But we all came. Of course he wasn't even ill."

"Did he upset anyone particularly during this visit?"

"He played his nasty jokes on all of us. I think perhaps that actress, Titchy Gold, was the worst affected." He told Hamish in detail of the original body-in-the-wardrobe trick, of Titchy's reaction to the headless knight. "Then she decided to flirt with him and the silly old goat fell for it. That was until, for some crazy reason, he decided to open up the seams in her best dresses. She went for him. He swore he didn't do it and he didn't find it funny, so perhaps he didn't."

"Do you know the terms of your brother's will?"

"No, I do not. I know the name of the firm of solicitors in Inverness that he used—Bright, Norton and Jiggs."

"Is it correct to assume that the bulk of his fortune would go to Charles, his adopted son? In Scotland, the man is always favoured in wills, even over real daughters."

"No, he detested Charles. He may have left it all to the cats' home as one last and great joke on the lot of us."

"Until the body is examined by the pathologist, we do not know the time of death. But if the body fell out on Titchy before she went to bed, and that was around midnight, and he had last been seen in the drawing-room at eleven o'clock, then it seems safe to assume he was killed between eleven and midnight. Where were you during that hour, Mr. Trent?"

"I? You surely don't think I would kill my own brother?"

Hamish waited patiently.

"Well, let me see. I had drinks with the others in the drawing-room. People kept coming and going. I myself went out to the library for a bit. I think it was just after Andrew went up to bed that Jan and I decided to retire."

"Was anyone missing from the drawing-room for a long time?"

"Titchy and Charles. They went outside, I mean outside the house, for a private talk."

"A full statement will be taken from you shortly. I'm just getting a few facts sorted out," said Hamish. "Would you send in the servants?"

After a few minutes Enrico and Maria appeared. Maria's eyes were red with weeping. "Name?" Hamish asked Enrico.

"Santos. Enrico Santos, and this is my wife, Maria."

"How long have you worked for Mr. Trent?"

"Fifteen years. Both of us."

"How did you find your way up here to the north of Scotland?"

"We were working in a restaurant in London," said Enrico in his careful and precise English. "It was owned by my father-in-law. We did not get on. Maria cannot have children and yet he blamed me. I saw an advertisement for a couple in *The Lady* magazine and we answered it. So we came to live with Mr. Trent."

"Do you both have British nationality now?"

"Of course."

"How long had you been in this country before you came up here?"

"Two years," said Enrico.

"Where are you from originally?"

"Barcelona. But," added Enrico proudly, "we now own two villas in Alicante which we rent out to holidaymakers."

"Mr. Trent must have paid good wages."

"He did." Enrico looked vaguely bored by all this questioning. "Our food and lodgings were paid for.

We do not smoke or drink. There is nothing to do up here. And so we invested our wages, made a profit, and bought property."

Hamish looked from Enrico to the downcast Maria. "But if you own property, why continue to work as servants for a difficult boss? What of all his practical jokes?"

"We were used to them," said Enrico with a shrug. "We wanted to leave but Mr. Trent said he had not long to live and he would leave us a lot of money in his will."

"Now to the murder," said Hamish. "Where were you both last night between eleven and midnight?"

"Mostly in the kitchen. We went up to the drawing-room about ten-thirty to make sure everyone had drinks and no one needed anything else and then we retired. I think by eleven-thirty we were in bed."

"Can you confirm this?" Hamish asked Maria.

She gave him a wide-eyed, frightened stare and then looked pleadingly at her husband, who said, "She confirms it."

"Tell me about when the body was found."

Enrico said that there had been a lot of loud screaming and shouting. He and Maria had been setting the breakfast table. They had run upstairs. Everyone was clustered round the body. Angela Trent said the police should be called immediately and went to do so. It had been assumed at first that the old man had fallen on the dagger during one of his practical jokes. No one but Miss Angela appeared to think it was murder at first.

"Now the main question. Why on earth was the body taken down and laid out? Surely you must know that nothing should have been touched."

Maria burst into a noisy flood of Spanish. Hamish caught the name Señora Trent.

"Which Trent was that?" he asked sharply.

"Mrs. Jeffrey," said Enrico. "She was most upset. She ran to look for her son and then came back and said it was horrible to leave Mr. Trent lying there. My wife is very religious. She wanted to lay out the body. I called in one of the gamekeepers, Jim Gaskell— he lives over the stables—and together we took Mr. Trent's body downstairs."

"Where is his shirt? The blood-stained one you took from the body?"

"Maria washed it. She did not know any better."

"But you must have known better!"

"I was in shock," said Enrico calmly.

"How busy you both were." Hamish leaned back in his chair and surveyed them. "You have aided and abetted the murderer by moving the body and cleaning Miss Gold's bedroom."

"It was Mrs. Jeffrey's suggestion," said Enrico. "She said there was no need to be slack about our duties and that the rooms needed cleaning as usual. With our master dead, we naturally took our orders from Mr. Jeffrey and his wife."

"Well, don't touch anything else. Send Mrs. Jeffrey in."

Anorexic? wondered Hamish, looking at Jan. She was wearing a black dress, short-sleeved, showing arms like sticks. Her face was gaunt and her rather protuberant eyes showed no traces of weeping.

"This is a waste of time," she began, sitting sideways on the very edge of a chair and crossing long thin legs. "Your superiors will soon be here and I see no reason to go through this ordeal twice."

Hamish ignored that.

"Why did you tell the servants to remove Mr. Trent's body?"

"I did not tell them *precisely* to do that. I simply said that it was dreadful to leave Andrew lying there. I mean, it may not be murder. Have you considered that? He may have been hiding in that wardrobe to scare Titchy and stabbed himself by accident."

"And the cleaning of the bedroom?"

"Again, I did not specifically tell them to clean that room. I merely said that they should get on with their duties. Servants must be kept up to the mark, you know," remarked Jan.

"How many servants do you have, Mrs. Trent?"

"I don't have any, but these are Spaniards and inherently lazy."

Hamish often wondered how the myth of the lazy Spaniard had arisen. In fact, he had been taught at school that the farther south you went, the lazier people got, and yet he had never seen any evidence to support that dubious fact.

In the Highlands and islands, it was another matter. He remembered when there had been another of those drives to bring work to the north and a factory had been opened on one of the Hebridean islands. It had not lasted very long. The workers had downed tools one day and walked out en masse, never to return. Their complaint was that a whistle had been blown to announce their tea-break and another whistle to signal time up. They did not like the sound of that whistle, they had said. The factory owner had damned them as lazy. Of course it could, on the other hand, be the quirky bloody-mindedness which was often the curse of the north.

"Tell me about your son, Paul," he said suddenly.

Jan went quite rigid.

"What about Paul?"

"Why did he leave?"

Jan shifted uncomfortably. "You saw his letter. It was these terrible practical jokes. No one in their right mind could stand them for very long."

"But you are still here."

Jan assumed an air of frankness. "You must know we all came here because Andrew said he was dying. A lie, as it turned out. But he is worth millions and quite capable of leaving it to that young fool, Charles. Paul is honest and upright and hard-working. I felt sure Andrew would be impressed by him."

"And was he?"

Jan laughed bitterly. "He was the same callous old fool he's always been."

"Tell me about Melissa Clarke."

"Some weird creature who works with Paul at the atomic research station. I think she ought to be investigated. Her clothes look lefty. She has pink hair. Pink hair, I ask you. As far as I could gather, this was the first time he had asked her anywhere. I think she is a corrupting influence."

"Your son being easily corrupted?"

"I didn't mean that. I meant, Paul is naïve and unworldly, thoroughly honest and straight. He thinks everyone else is the same."

"Where were you between eleven and midnight last night?"

"I was in the drawing-room."

"Did you leave it at any time?"

"I went up at one point to . . . er . . . use the bathroom."

"Before Mr. Trent retired to bed or after?"

"I can't remember."

"That will do for now. Send in Miss Gold."

Titchy Gold had changed into a low-cut black blouse and long dark skirt. She seemed nervously excited.

"Miss Gold," said Hamish. "I will need to take you through this again. I want you to tell me all about your visit from the beginning."

Titchy gave him a competent and brief summary

of everything that had happened, right to the finding of the body.

"There is just one thing," said Hamish, "you said you were talking outside to Charles Trent for a long time. What about?"

Titchy fluttered her eyelashes. "Come now, Constable, what do lovers usually talk about?"

"Yet you say he joined you in your bed later. Would that not have been a more comfortable place to discuss things?"

"Hardly, copper. We were otherwise occupied."

"Is Titchy Gold your real name?"

"Yes. Quaint, isn't it? Mummy and Daddy were Shakespearian actors."

"I cannae call to mind a Titchy Gold anywhere in Shakespeare."

Titchy gave a musical laugh. "Silly. I mean they were bohemian, extravagant people. It was just like them to think up an odd name for me."

"Where are they now?"

"Both dead."

"Of what?"

"They died in the Paris air crash of '82."

Titchy whipped out a handkerchief and dabbed her eyes.

I don't like this woman one bit, thought Hamish suddenly.

"When is the will being read?" demanded Titchy suddenly.

"That I do not know. Strathbane police will no doubt call the solicitors in Inverness and ask them to send someone here. Why? Surely you do not hope to inherit?" asked Hamish, being deliberately stupid.

"No, but Charles will. He must. He's the son."

"Adopted. Besides, Mr. Jeffrey says that Mr. Andrew Trent may have planned his last joke by leaving the lot to a cats' home."

Something unlovely flashed in Titchy's eyes and was gone. "Any more questions?"

"Not for now. Send in Miss Angela Trent."

Despite her mannish appearance, Angela Trent was the first one of them, apart from Maria, that Hamish had met who seemed distressed.

"I will not keep you long," he said gently. "Where were you last night between eleven and midnight?"

She looked at him in genuine bewilderment. "The drawing-room. I suppose. Oh, I went down to the kitchen and asked Enrico to bring up some sandwiches because Dad said he wanted some, brown bread and smoked salmon. Then I was a bit upset. I went up to my room and sat down for a little. You see, there had been all those jokes and rows and then that little actress accused Dad of having cut up her dresses and she was so mad she looked as if she could have killed him."

Hamish gave an exclamation. He ran to the door and shouted for Enrico and when the manservant arrived he told him to tell Miss Gold not to touch any of the clothes that had been damaged. Forensic would want to examine them.

He returned to Angela, who had heard the exchange and looked pale.

"It's amazing what they can get fingerprints from these days," said Hamish. "Now, Miss Trent. Who, in your opinion, would want to kill your father?"

She shook her head in a bewildered way and then her eyes hardened.

"That cheap actress."

"Titchy Gold? Why?"

"Because she's going to marry Charles. She thinks Charles will inherit. That low, common sort of person would do anything."

"What were your relations with your father?"

"A trifle strained," said Angela gruffly. "It was those jokes of his, you know. Sewed the bottoms of my pyjama legs together and punctured Betty's hot-water bottle. He'd always played tricks on us, even when we were small."

He asked her several more questions about where the other guests had been during the crucial time and then asked to see Betty.

Betty Trent looked small and crushed and mousy. Angela had found a dark blouse and skirt to wear, but Betty was wearing a pink wool twin set with a green tweed skirt. She said she had been in and out of the drawing-room and could not remember exact times. She said she did not believe her father had been murdered. He had meant to play a trick and the heavy door of the wardrobe had slammed on him and driven the knife into him. She said she estimated that P.C. Macbeth was in his thirties and if a policeman was in his thirties and had not yet been promoted, it showed he was a village hick with no brains at all. Furthermore, she would not waste any more time with him, but would wait for his superiors.

"Chust a minute," said Hamish. "Who do you think cut Miss Gold's frocks?"

"Probably Dad," said Betty crossly, "although I must admit it was a new departure in jokes."

Hamish was about to take her through the finding of the body more out of sheer bloody-mindedness than anything else, for Betty's remarks had riled him, when the noise of a helicopter filled the air.

The police from Strathbane had arrived.

Detective Chief Inspector Blair was a heavy-set Glaswegian. Hamish had worked with him before. Blair knew Hamish had solved several cases in the past and had allowed Blair to take the credit. But every time he saw Hamish again, he convinced himself it had all really been luck on Hamish's part. This lanky gormless Highlander could surely not compete with the sharper brains of a Lowland Scot. Blair was flanked by his pet detectives, Jimmy Anderson and Harry MacNab.

"Came by the chopper," said Blair and settled himself into an easy chair in the library with a grunt. "So the auld fart his bin knifed."

"You knew him?" asked Hamish.

"Heard o' him and his damp jokes. Forensic's on the way. Right, laddie, let's have whit you've got."

Hamish took out his notebook and Blair guffawed with laughter. "Have ye never heard o' a tape recorder? How did ye get here? On a bike wi' square stone wheels?"

Hamish ignored him and began to read out the brief statements he had taken. Blair listened intently. When Hamish had finished, Blair slapped his knee and exclaimed, "Man, man, you've got your murderers!"

"Who?"

"Them Spaniards, o' course. Always sticking knives into people. They destroyed the evidence, didn't they? They hope to inherit. Anderson, get on to thae lawyers in Inverness and get one o' them up here fast. I bet the pair of them get a chunk o' the old man's money in that will."

Hamish groaned inwardly. Blair, he knew, had a deep mistrust of all foreigners. "Look, they're both very correct servants," said Hamish. "They've been in this country for a long time. They speak English better than you..."

"Just watch your lip, laddie."

"I would also advise you to go easy on the racist

remarks you usually make about foreigners," said Hamish firmly. "Enrico could easily get you in trouble. He's no fool."

"You mean the Race Relations Board," sneered Blair. "That lot o' Commies don't know their arse from their elbow. I'm no' scared o' them. Furthermair, whit's a village bobby doing advising me? Bugger off, Sherlock, and leave me to wrap this up."

Hamish walked stiffly from the room. If, just if, he solved this case, then he would go out of his way to expose Blair for the crass fool he was. But, said a voice in his head, that would mean promotion and leaving Lochdubh and your cosy life.

When Enrico was summoned again to the library, his sharp dark eyes ranged about the room. "Speaka da English?" asked Blair with heavy irony.

"I am looking for the tape recorder," said Enrico. "This is, I take it, the official interview. So it should be recorded."

"You listen tae me, you cheeky pillock," roared Blair. "I'll conduct this interview any way I like and any more complaints from you and I'll have you deported."

"You cannot," pointed out Enrico. "I am a British citizen, as is my wife."

Blair launched into a series of bullying haranguing questions punctuated with insults about greasy Spaniards. Enrico answered when he could and what he could and then got to his feet. "I hivnae finished," roared Blair.

"I think I had better leave you to consider your manner and behaviour," said Enrico. He took a tape recorder out of his pocket. "*I* have recorded this interview. Unless you conduct yourself in a polite manner, this tape will go to your superiors at Strathbane."

Blair's eyes bulged with fury. Jimmy Anderson stepped forward. "Run along," he said to Enrico. "We'll call you when we want you again."

"Jeezus," groaned Blair.

"Aye," said Jimmy, "can you imagine what Superintendent Daviot would say when he heard that? He'd kick ye out so hard, you'd be skidding on your bum frae here to Glasgow."

"Well, you know whit tae do," growled Blair. "We're going tae search all the rooms, right? Get that tape and wipe it out!"

Hamish went up to Titchy's bedroom. The forensic team had arrived. Men in white boiler suits were dusting for prints and cutting little bits off the pile of the carpet near the wardrobe. "Could the body have been killed somewhere else," Hamish asked one, "and then put in the wardrobe?"

"Could be," said the man. "It would take more than one person or a very strong man. You see, the fact that the body remained upright, propped against the closed door either meant that he had been killed earlier somewhere else and rigor had set in, or that the narrow confines of the wardrobe kept the body supported until Miss Gold opened the door."

"I don't think there was time for rigor to set in," said Hamish. "Maybe Titchy Gold actually saw a dummy before she went to bed and someone killed the old man during the night and substituted his body for the dummy. But she'd need to be a verra heavy sleeper."

He turned away and almost bumped into Jimmy Anderson, who was grinning all over his narrow foxy face. "Blair says you're to help in the search, starting wi' the servants' room."

"Meaning he's put his foot in it with Enrico?"

"Aye. He bashed on like the bigot he is and the wee Spaniard taped the lot and is threatening to send it to Daviot if Blair doesn't toe the line."

Hamish went downstairs and met Enrico in the hall and asked him to take him to the quarters he shared with his wife.

Enrico led him down to the basement. He and Maria shared two rooms beside the games room, a bedroom and a small living-room. He stood in the doorway and watched Hamish. "If you are looking for that tape," said Enrico, "I have it in my pocket."

"And I'd keep it there," said Hamish with a grin. Enrico waited while Hamish carefully went through drawers and cupboards. "I'm only the first," said Hamish. "The forensic team will go through everything as well, including the kitchen. You'd better check your knives and see if any are missing."

"I have already done so," said Enrico. "A jointing knife is missing."

"When did you discover that?" demanded Hamish.

"Earlier on. It was the first thing I looked for."

"Why didn't you tell me or Blair?"

"I found it after my interview with you and before my interview with Mr. Blair. Had he treated me with more courtesy, I would have told him."

Hamish shook his head. "You cannae go around questioning the niceties of police behaviour in the middle o' a murder inquiry."

"No?" Enrico patted the pocket of his dark jacket which held the tape. "When Mr. Blair calms down, he will realize that anyone in this house could have taken the knife from the kitchen at any time. I did not have any birds to joint in the last couple of days, so it could have been missing at any time during that period."

Hamish looked around the living-room again. It was neat and clean but somehow characterless: three-piece suite, coffee table, bookshelves with some magazines and paperbacks, and two pot plants. Above the fireplace was a framed photograph of the Ramblas, the main street in Barcelona.

"You said your wife was very religious," said Hamish slowly. "But there are no religious paintings here, no crucifix, no religious statues."

"I said my wife was religious," said Enrico. "I am not."

Hamish looked thoughtfully at him. Enrico's dark brown eyes looked blandly back.

"I'll be talking to you later," said Hamish.

He went up to the library and told the furious Blair about the knife and about the fact that there was no way of getting that tape. "I don't think Enrico will send it off unless you start accusing him of deliberately tampering with the evidence—which you could have done," said Hamish, "if you hadn't put his back up. There's one thing you could do, however."

"And whit's that?"

"Get Mrs. Jeffrey Trent in here and accuse her of having paid the servants to lay out the body and clean the room."

Blair goggled at Hamish.

"Aye," said Hamish. "A guess. But a good one, I think. Enrico and Maria are not the sort to become sentimental about the death o' their late master. They're hard-headed. They already own property in Alicante and it's my belief they'll leave after the reading of the will, no matter who is the new master or mistress here. It was only hope of getting something in that will that kept them here. When the body was discovered, Mrs. Jeffrey ran straight to her son's room and found him gone. For some reason, she's protecting him. The reason could be that she's simply a rather neurotic and possessive mother."

"Oh, well, I'll give it a try," said Blair sulkily.

"And make it official," said Hamish. "Recorder and all."

When Jan came into the library, Blair, Anderson and Hamish were there and there was an official tape recorder on the desk in front of Blair.

"How much did you pay Enrico to lay out the body and clean the room?" demanded Blair.

She went a muddy colour. "Who says I paid them?"

Hamish's quiet Highland voice interrupted. "It will be easy to find out. Whatever it was, I doubt if you would have that amount of ready cash on you. So you would give him a cheque—a cheque which will show up at your bank."

"I want a lawyer," she said faintly.

"Mrs. Jeffrey Trent," intoned Blair, "I must warn you that you have a right to remain silent, but everything you say will be taken down and may be used in evidence against you."

She suddenly collapsed and began to cry. Through gulps and sobs, she said she was overwrought. She had not been trying to protect Paul. She thought old Andrew had died because of a joke that had gone wrong. That was her story and she was sticking to it.

When she was finally allowed to leave, Blair said with satisfaction, "I've got that bloody Spaniard now. Taking money to pervert the course o' justice."

"And he hass still got you," said Hamish. "He's got that tape."

Blair swore viciously.

Then the phone rang. It was the Inverness police. Paul Sinclair and Melissa Clarke had been picked up at Inverness station and were being brought back to Arrat House.

Melissa had never been so happy. She was sitting on a red plastic seat in Inverness station beside Paul. The London train was almost due to arrive.

They had skied across country as far as Lairg, where they had taken the train to Inverness. After arranging for the skis to be sent back, they had gone for lunch and had joked and laughed and giggled like schoolchildren.

They would come back to the Highlands on their honeymoon, thought Melissa dreamily. Although Paul had not proposed marriage, she was sure he would, some time in the near future. Her mind was filled with glorious images of snow-covered moorland and soaring mountains. She felt tired and happy and her face still tingled from the exercise and the cold, biting air.

Policemen came into the station, policemen of various ranks. Two guarded the entrance. Melissa watched them with that rather smug curiosity of the law-abiding watching the police looking for some malefactor.

Her wool ski cap was suddenly making her head feel itchy. She pulled it off and her pink hair shone under the station lights.

And then all the police veered in their direction.

An inspector stood before them. "Paul Sinclair and Melissa Clarke?" he asked.

Paul blinked up through his glasses. "Yes, that's us. What's up? Has anything happened to Mother?"

"You are to accompany us," said the inspector stonily.

Bewildered, they rose to their feet. Two policemen relieved them of their rucksacks. They walked out of the station. A white police car was waiting in the forecourt. They got in the back. A thin policewoman got in beside them and two policemen in the front. The car sped off.

"What is this?" demanded Melissa. "What has happened?"

The man in the front passenger seat slewed round. "Mr. Andrew Trent was found murdered this morning at Arrat House. We are taking you back there for questioning."

Paul buried his face in his hands.

"But what has his death to do with us?" protested Melissa. "We left at dawn this morning."

"Although the body was found this morning," said the policeman, "it is estimated that Mr. Trent was killed the night before."

"How ... how was he killed?"

"He was stabbed to death. Now, if you've any more questions, put them to Detective Chief Inspector Blair, who is in charge of the investigations at

Arrat House." He turned to the driver. "No use taking the Struie Pass in this weather, Jamie. You'd best go round by the coast."

Paul remained huddled up, his face still in his hands. Melissa shivered with dread. What did she know of him? What did she know of any of them? The countryside which had seemed so glorious in the morning sunlight now looked alien and forbidding, bleak and white in the headlights of the police car.

Back to Arrat House. Back to where among those overheated rooms was a murderer. She reached out to put an arm around Paul and then shrank back. The man she had been dreaming about getting married to was now a stranger to her.

Chapter Four

*It requires a surgical operation to get a joke
well into a Scotch understanding.*

—The Reverend Sydney Smith

While Melissa and Paul were speeding on their way
back to Arrat House, Hamish was sitting quietly in
the library, listening to Blair interviewing Charles
Trent.

The young man interested him. He was surely old
Andrew Trent's heir. Charles was saying that Andrew
had adopted him while he, Charles, was still a baby.
No, he said amiably, he didn't know who his real parents were, and had never been curious.

What had his relationship with the dead man been
like? Charles looked serious, opened his mouth to
say something, and then shrugged. "Why pretend?"
he said. "He despised me. It seemed I couldn't do a
thing right as far as he was concerned. I wanted to go

into the business instead of going up to Oxford, but he said nastily it was a successful business and I would probably ruin it. He did all right by me in material ways, best school and all that, but I never remember him particularly wanting to have me around. I'm not upset by his death . . . yet. The shock is still too great, so I don't know whether I am going to grieve or not."

"Did you speak to him at all just before he died?"

"No, I was out in the snow, talking to my fiancée."

"With whom you spent the night?"

"Gosh, did she tell you that? Yes."

"And when you went to her room, didn't you see the body?"

"No, the room was in shadow apart from a little pool of light from a lamp beside the bed. I looked at Titchy, you see. I didn't look anywhere else."

"What were you and Miss Gold talking about?" asked Hamish suddenly.

"Well, lovers' talk, you know, things like that."

"Why did you go outside in the cold?"

"Needed a breath of fresh air. This house is always overheated. When will I know what's in the will?"

"Tomorrow," said Blair. "About eleven o'clock provided the roads stay clear."

When Charles had left, Blair rounded on Hamish.

"Why were you so interested in what he was talking about?"

"I just wondered," said Hamish, "whether they might have been quarrelling. I mean, he brought her up here and she must know it was because he hoped the old man was really dying. It turns out he's not. She gets awful jokes played on her and then her dresses are cut. Charles Trent got a modest yearly allowance from Mr. Andrew Trent. So he had to work but he doesn't seem to be able to keep a job for long or get a successful one. I wondered if maybe Titchy had decided to dump him."

"It's an idea," admitted Blair ungraciously. "But mark my words, that Jan Trent knows Paul Sinclair did it. It's jist a matter o' breaking him down."

Hamish stifled a sigh. Blair's bullying methods rarely got him anywhere but he never seemed to understand that.

"What are you going to do about Enrico?" he asked maliciously.

"I'll deal wi' that one in my ain good time," snarled Blair. "Look, why don't you shove off, Hamish? It's getting late. I'll see this Paul Sinclair and his girl and then start again tomorrow. We'll have the will and the autopsy report then."

Hamish knew Blair wanted to be rid of him because the detective was sure that Paul Sinclair was the murderer and he didn't want Hamish around to share in the credit.

He walked out of the library and collected his overcoat from a peg in the hall. Then he heard a scrunch of car wheels on frozen snow and went outside.

Melissa and Paul had arrived. Paul was white-faced.

Melissa looked tired and scared. Hamish watched as they were ushered inside. He felt sorry for them. Blair would give them both a hard time of it.

He drove slowly homeward, the great bright stars of Sutherland burning fiercely overhead. The roads had been gritted and salted but were beginning to freeze in a hard frost.

The police station would be freezing cold, he thought gloomily. Maybe if he could solve this murder, he would offer Blair the credit in return for a suggestion to police headquarters that central heating was installed. Instead of going straight home, he turned into the drive leading to Tommel Castle Hotel. Landowner Colonel Halburton-Smythe had turned his home into an hotel after he had lost a great deal of money. The suggestion had come from Hamish. The hotel had quickly become a great success, but the colonel never gave Hamish Macbeth any credit for the idea, perhaps because he frowned on the village bobby's friendship with his daughter Priscilla.

The guests had finished dining and were having their coffee in the hotel lounge, formerly the castle drawing-room. Jenkins, once butler, now maître d', frowned at the sight of Hamish, for Jenkins was a snob, but reluctantly said that Priscilla could be found in the bar. The bar was in a room off the entrance hall. What had it been before? wondered Hamish, trying to remember. Priscilla was behind the bar checking some accounts.

"Still working?" said Hamish. "I thought now that Mr. Johnson had taken over as hotel manager you would be able to lead a life of ease."

"There's still a lot to do," said Priscilla, shutting a ledger with a firm bang. "Besides, the barman's off with flu—not that the bar gives me much work. This party of guests like their drinks in the lounge and the waiters cope with that. Mr. Johnson and I have finally talked Daddy into getting a computer for the accounts. Have a whisky on the house, and tell me your news."

Hamish watched her as she poured him a shot of whisky. She was as cool, blonde and competent as ever in a severe black dress and black high heels.

"I refuse to stand behind the bar any longer," said Priscilla with a sigh. "It's been a long day. Let's take our drinks over to the table at the window. If anyone comes in, I'll get Jenkins to find one of the waiters to take over."

"The morning-room," exclaimed Hamish. "I couldnae remember what room this used to be."

"Changed times," said Priscilla. "We're making money hand over fist and we're booked up all year round, but if I suggest to Daddy that he might now go back to being lord of the manor, he turns green at the gills with fright. Losing that money scared the hell out of him. What brings you here?"

"I wanted to see you," said Hamish, remembering briefly the time when he had been so much in love with her that he would have been unable to say anything as honest as that. "Besides, I've got a murder. Arrat House. I've been there all day. It was the thought o' going back to that freezing police station, apart from wanting to see you, that brought me here."

"Where's Towser?" asked Priscilla. Towser was Hamish's dog.

"At the station, but Priscilla, that animal doesn't feel the cold."

"Hamish, you are so lazy! A fire takes no time to get going. Drink up and we'll both go to the station and warm that poor dog and feed it."

"Towser can look after himself," pleaded Hamish, but Priscilla replied that she was going to fetch her coat.

Proof that the mongrel could indeed take care of itself was discovered when they found Towser snuggled down under the blankets on Hamish's bed. Hamish wanted to tell her about the case but had to wait until she had lit the kitchen stove and prepared food for Towser.

"Now," she said, "that's better," and Hamish wondered again how it was that someone so elegant and with such a pampered upbringing should have turned out to be such an efficient housekeeper.

He told her all about the murder and she listened intently. "You see," finished Hamish "there's one thing I'm sure of. Not one of them knew what was in that will. If just one of them looked or sounded as if they knew and if that someone turned out to be the beneficiary, then I think I would find the murderer."

"You mean, his millions are the reason for the murder?"

"What else?"

"Well, his jokes, Hamish. You've forgotten something. He played jokes on people in the village as well. They hated him like poison. Everyone knows that."

Hamish's stomach rumbled and he coughed to conceal the noise. He was hungry, but if Priscilla knew that, she would start clattering pots and pans to make him a meal and he wanted to discuss the case.

"Aye, that's right," he said slowly. "Mind you, someone would need to be a lunatic to kill him over a joke."

"There are jokes and jokes," said Priscilla. "He might have humiliated someone quite dreadfully and you Highlanders are a terribly touchy lot."

"I'll go over to the village in the morning," said Hamish.

"Is Blair allowing you in on this case?"

"For the moment. I'm covering MacGregor's patch, oo I have every right to be there."

Priscilla leaned forward. "Is it any use pointing out to you that promotion would mean more comfort? If you like it so much here, why didn't you rush back to feed your dog instead of coming to the hotel?"

"I told you," said Hamish stiffly, "I wanted tae

see you. Iss there anything wrong in that, Miss Halburton-Smythe?"

She studied him thoughtfully and then gave a rueful smile. "I should be flattered, Hamish Macbeth, but I happen to know you are a moocher."

"Well, if you want to think I wass after the free drink and the free heat, that iss your damned business."

Priscilla stared at him in amazement. He coloured but turned his head away and sat with his arms folded.

"I'm off," she said suddenly. "It's a good thing I brought my own car. Call on me again when you're over your sulks."

Hamish felt like a fool when she had gone. What on earth had possessed him to snap at her like that? His stomach gave another rumble. That was it. He was hungry. It was not as if he were still in love with Priscilla and sensitive to her every remark. But he shouldn't have left Towser behind in the freezing cold. He would take the dog with him in the morning.

Titchy Gold and Charles Trent were snuggled up in bed, his bedroom, Titchy's being still sealed off. "So you didn't mean that about leaving me," said Charles.

"Silly," she giggled. "I was out of my mind with all those hellish jokes."

Charles clasped his hands behind his head and

stared up at the ceiling. "I just hope you aren't pinning your hopes on that will. I'm not."

"Oh, yes, you are," said Titchy. "You've been strung up all day."

Charles gave a reluctant laugh. "Terrible, isn't it? But I am his son and so he's got to leave me the bulk of it."

And at that remark, Titchy ended the conversation by becoming very amorous indeed.

Along the corridor in their room, Betty and Angela Trent lay awake. Betty kept snivelling dismally and the tip of her nose was pink.

"I don't know why you're so upset," complained Angela. "I mean, we were both shocked at first, but it's good in a way to be rid of him and it's no use pretending otherwise."

Betty shivered. "That's a sinful thought. Do you believe there is a hell, Angela?"

"No, but then I don't believe in heaven either."

Betty shifted restlessly. "I suppose Charles will get the bulk of the money and then he'll marry that little tart and *she'll* get her claws into it."

"Just hope he's left *us* something," said Angela, "or we'll be in real trouble."

Jeffrey was striding up and down his bedroom, berating his wife, an odd state of affairs, for in their marriage it was usually the other way around. "What on earth possessed you to get the servants to take the body away and clean up?" he kept asking. "You dote on that boy of yours and yet you've landed him in terrible trouble and all because you were frightened he had done it. You must be mad. That wimp couldn't kill anyone."

Jan found her voice. "Don't you dare criticize my son," she said in a thin voice. "At least he earns decent money, which is more than I can say for you."

"I was earning very good money when you married me," pointed out Jeffrey acidly. "I am not responsible for the recession in this country."

"You're responsible for a lot of hare-brained deals. Pinky told me." Pinky was a colleague's wife.

"So that's your idea of loyalty? Gossiping about me behind my back? Poking into my affairs? I could wring your scrawny neck."

"Try it," she jeered. "Just try it."

"Oh, shut up, you bitch," he muttered, suddenly weary. He climbed into the double bed beside her and both lay as stiff as boards, not touching, each plotting ways on how best to hurt the other. I've still got my looks, thought Jan, to whom extreme thinness was beauty. If he doesn't get any money in that will, then I'll find someone else.

Jeffrey thought, If I don't get any money, I'll take everything we've got left and disappear to Spain. That'd serve the bitch right. She might even have to find out what it's like to work for a living. In the last few years, failure and frustration had taught him to hate. He now hated his wife every bit as much as he had hated his brother. He forced himself to relax. In his mind's eye, he lay on a Spanish beach in the blazing sunshine while a buxom Spanish girl with bobbing breasts and not one anorexic bone showing brought him a long cool drink.

Melissa was sick for the second time that evening. Sweating and shivering, she climbed into bed. She would never, even in her left-wing days, have believed the police could be such pigs. She could still see Blair's face, bloated with rage as he hurled questions at her and Paul. And a fat lot of good Paul had been. He had cringed before Blair, apologized for his very existence on this planet, thought Melissa savagely.

Blair had turned over her whole life, her family, her career, and he had obviously regarded her pink hair as a sure sign she took drugs. Good God! He had even got that thin policewoman from Inverness to examine her arms for needle marks. And she had been so happy just that morning, so free, planning a life with Paul. A fat tear rolled down her nose and plopped on the sheet.

Down in his living-room, Enrico sat with his pocket calculator and his bank books and counted his savings. "We've done very well," he said in Spanish to his wife, not the lisping Spanish of the south but a hard Catalan accent. "We'll wait to see what's in that will and then we'll leave. Hey, Maria, back to Spain after all these years in exile. We can live like grandees."

Maria gave him a placid smile. Whatever Enrico did or said was right.

Paul Sinclair crept along to his mother's room and slowly pushed open the door. Jeffrey Trent was asleep but he could see the glitter of his mother's eyes in the darkness. "Paul," she whispered. She got out of bed, wrapped herself in a dressing-gown and ran to him. He went into her arms and she held him tightly.

"Let's find somewhere where we can talk," she said urgently. "We've got to talk."

Next morning, Hamish Macbeth ambled up the village street of Arrat with his dog at his heels. He remembered a Mrs. King who lived in the main street. She had once lived in Lochdubh and was an excellent source of gossip. He knocked at the door of her cottage and waited patiently. Mrs. King, he knew, was crippled with arthritis. At last the door creaked open and Mrs. King peered up at him. She had a face like an elderly toad. "Why, Hamish," she said. "It iss yourself. Come ben."

He followed her into her small cramped living-room. Towser stretched out in front of the fire and went to sleep.

"It iss the murder that has brought ye," said Mrs. King. "My, my, the auld scunner deserved tae be kilt, and the good Lord forgive me for saying so. The pressmen haff arrived and they are looking for places to stay. That Mrs. Angus, her doon the road, hass let her ain bedroom to two fellows from *The Sun*, but I wouldnae stoop tae such a thing."

Mrs. King looked wistful, all the same.

"Tell me," said Hamish, "is there anyone in Arrat itself who hated the auld man? Is there anyone who had such a nasty joke played on him that he might kill?"

She folded her deformed hands on top of the handle of her stick and rested her chins on them. "Aye," she said at last. "But it wass twa year gone."

"We have the long memories in the Highlands when it comes to insults," said Hamish. "Who was it? What happened?"

She half-closed her reptilian eyes. "It wass the gamekeeper up at the big hoose, Jim Gaskell, what lives in the flat above the stables wi' his family."

Hamish listened in horror as the story unfolded. Jim's wife had had a baby two years ago in a hospital in Inverness. Jim had not been allowed to go to the hospital because Mr. Trent was complaining about poachers on his land and did not want an absent gamekeeper but said he would send Enrico with the car to bring home wife and baby. Jim came in from the hill one day to be told that his wife and new baby were home and waiting for him. His wife, Mary, proudly led him into the little spare bedroom they had turned into a nursery. They approached the cradle and Mary gently pulled back the covers. They found themselves staring down at a small chimpanzee wearing a baby's bonnet. Mary had fainted with shock and had struck her head on a chest of drawers as she went down and suffered a severe concussion. Jim found old Andrew Trent hiding in the next room, holding the shrieking baby, and laughing fit to burst. Jim had threatened to kill Andrew, but then it was rumoured that Andrew had paid over money for the baby's upkeep and so it had all died down.

Hamish sat turning this over in his mind. No Highlander would ever forgive a thing like that. But knifing in such a way? A bullet through Andrew Trent's brain as the old man was walking through his estates would have been more the way Jim would have killed him.

"Anyone else?" Hamish asked and then listened to a catalogue of the old man's jokes, from putting a cat in the school piano before the annual concert to nailing up the doors of Jean Macleod's cottage on her wedding day and making the frantic girl and her family late for church. What a power money was, thought Hamish in amazement. Had Andrew Trent been poor, his family would probably have had him certified as dangerously mad long ago.

He thanked the old woman and went up towards Arrat House with Towser. A group of shivering men and women, like refugees, were huddled outside the gates. The press had arrived.

He politely told them all to put any questions to Blair and walked up the drive. As he was approaching the house, he saw a girl in front of him, a girl with pink hair. "Miss Clarke," he called.

Melissa swung round, saw Hamish's uniform, and turned pale.

"It's all right," he said easily. "I am not going to question you at the moment." She had beautiful eyes, he noticed, well spaced and dark grey. He thought her pink hair suited her. "Did Blair give you a hard time?" he asked.

Melissa looked up at him warily but the policeman's hazel eyes were kind and his ridiculous-looking dog was slowly wagging its plume of a tail.

"Yes, very," she said in a low voice.

"It was because you went away," said Hamish. "He wasn't really after you but Paul Sinclair. You see, Paul's mother, Mrs. Trent, paid the servants to take away the body and clean the room. So Blair figured that the mother knew the son had done it and was covering up the evidence."

"It was awful," said Melissa. "I didn't know the police could be like that. You know, at university,

I was in some left-wing groups and they called the police fascist pigs, but I never quite believed it until now. I was brought up in a family which always went to the police when in trouble."

"Blair's in a class of his own," said Hamish. "Wait until the will is read and he'll be after the beneficiaries. He cannot keep you here much longer, you know. Give it another day and then you can leave your address and go back home."

They had reached the house. Melissa drew back. "I don't want to go in," she said in a shaky voice.

Hamish looked up at the sky. The sun was shining and there was a hint of warmth in the air. The mountain above the house was sharp-edged against the sky, like a cut-out. A pair of buzzards sailed lazily in the clear air.

He turned away from the house and she fell into step beside him. "I want to ask you a question," said Hamish, his accent suddenly stronger, more Highland, more sibilant, as it always became when he was nervous.

"Must you?" said Melissa. "I've had enough of questions."

"It iss not about the case. Do you see this dog, Towser?"

Melissa looked down in surprise at the great yellowish mongrel, who gave her a doggy grin. "Yes, of course, I see him."

"I wass here all the day long yesterday because of

the murder; I left this animal locked up in the police station all day. The police station iss cold, mind you. He had been fed in the morning and had plenty of water. But on the road home, I couldnae bear the idea of going straight back to a cold house and so I dropped in on a friend whose family hass the big hotel. This friend, she said I wass cruel to leave the dog so long."

Melissa looked up at him in sudden amusement. "Are you asking me whether I thought you were cruel?"

"Yes," said Hamish.

"Well," said Melissa cautiously, "what about walks? Was Towser there all day without a walk?"

"No, Mrs. Wellington, the minister's wife, has the key, and she walked him in the morning and the afternoon."

"No, I don't think you are cruel. Your dog has a pampered look. You are not really like a policeman, you know."

"I am verra like a policeman," said Hamish huffily. "Mair like one than that great bullying fathead inside." A car swept by them. "The lawyer," exclaimed Hamish. "I must hear this."

Melissa found herself trotting after him as he headed back to the house with long strides. He emanated a sort of sane kindness, she thought. "Could you look after Towser for me?" asked Hamish. "See if Enrico can give him a bone or something."

Melissa took Towser's leash, glad of the dog's company, glad of a chore to do which would keep her away from Paul. "Enrico will be at the reading as well," she said cheerfully, "so Towser and I will raid the larder."

Hamish eased himself into the library and stood at the back. They were all there, tense and eager. Not a dry eye in the house, he thought cynically, but then Andrew Trent did not deserve grief or mourning.

The lawyer, Mr. Bright, seemed determined to live up to his name. He was a small fat man with round glasses and an air of determined cheerfulness.

He began by making a speech about what an amazingly fun-loving person the dear deceased had been, about how his japes and pranks had delighted all, while the roomful of relatives and police listened in stony silence.

Hamish was almost prepared to find out that this will was Andrew Trent's last great joke on his family. But as the will was read out, it transpired that there was only one disaster.

Charles was to inherit absolutely nothing.

Andrew Trent had left instructions that his house, estates and factories were to be sold. The proceeds, along with his money in the bank, were to be divided equally among his daughters, Angela and Betty, his brother, Jeffrey, and, surprisingly, Paul Sinclair. Generous bequests had been left to the Spanish servants and outdoor staff, including Jim Gaskell.

Charles was quite white with shock. He reached for Titchy's hand. Titchy seemed as stunned as Charles.

The rest were obviously finding it very hard to control their glee. Freedom at last, thought Jeffrey. I'll leave the bitch to rot. Her son can take care of her if he wants.

Hamish noticed that Blair had a gloating look which he recognized of old. Blair obviously thought he knew the identity of the murderer.

When everyone had finally filed out, leaving the police behind, Hamish turned to Blair. "You've found something," he said.

"You've found something, *sir,*" corrected Blair nastily. "Aye, it's in the bag. We'll have her in here in a minute."

"Her?"

"So-called Titchy Gold. We've been getting background fast. Take a look at this. Good thing the old man's got a fax machine."

Hamish read it curiously. Titchy Gold had been born plain Martha Brown, mother Mrs. Enid Brown, late father, Terence Brown, unemployed. Titchy, or Martha, had appeared in the juvenile court at the age of fourteen. She had stabbed her father to death. The reason she had stabbed him was because he had raped her. She had served a short sentence in a juvenile detention centre. She had never gone home again and refused to have anything to do with her mother. At eighteen, she had become the mistress of a television producer, changed her name by deed poll and started getting small parts, ending up with the plum part in the present crime series in which she appeared.

Hamish raised his eyes. "There iss a lot of difference between stabbing a father who's raped you and stabbing an old man you hardly know."

"When they start killing, they go on killing," said Blair, rubbing his fat hands. "She thought Charles Trent would inherit, didn't she? Ye can sit in on the interview, Hamish," he added magnanimously.

Hamish hesitated. He felt he ought to tell Blair about the gamekeeper, Jim Gaskell. Then he decided it would be better if he questioned Jim Gaskell himself first.

"No, I'll leave it to you," said Hamish. He could not bear to see the bullying and haranguing that would go on. But he privately thought Blair was in for a surprise. Titchy Gold was much harder and tougher than the detective knew.

And so it turned out. Blair was sweating by the time Titchy had finished with him. She used the foulest language he had ever heard in his life. She reminded him that she was a celebrity and that the press were outside. She would let them know about his methods of interviewing and no doubt some television research team would be interested in questioning *him*. She did not deny a thing in the report. Her father had been a degenerate. She had carved a career for herself and no one was going to take that away from her. She ended by saying that he either charged her and produced immediate evidence for doing so, or let her go, or she would get a lawyer flown up from London to sort him out. Furthermore, she was packing her bags and leaving the next day.

Hamish stood for a moment outside the library door, listening with relish to the noisy altercation from within, and then he went out in search of Jim Gaskell.

The gamekeeper and his wife were both at home. Mary Gaskell was just putting the infant down to sleep.

Hamish talked easily of this and that and then slid round to the question of practical jokes. "That was a bad business about the baby," he said. "Did you know he was leaving you something in his will?"

"I neffer thocht it for a minute," said Jim.

"But you obviously know now. You're not surprised. Who told you?"

"Enrico. The wee Spaniard came running right over tae tell me."

"But you didn't know before. Mr. Trent didn't say anything?"

"Of course he did. He was aye telling me and Enrico and the others that we'd come in for a bit, but only Enrico believed him."

"You must have been sore angry at him over that joke he played on you."

"I could hae killed him," said the gamekeeper simply, his large powerful hands resting on his knees. He was a giant of a man. "But I got my revenge."

"How?"

"Blackmail," said the gamekeeper with a cheery grin. "I had Mary here right down tae Inverness tae the lawyers and doctors and psychiatrists and then I told auld Trent I wass going tae sue him. Danger tae Mary's health, shock, trauma, the lot. He settled out o' court."

"For how much?"

"Ten thousand pounds. I'm no' a greedy man. After that, every time he wanted help wi' one o' his jokes, I'd charge him a fee. It was me that wass the headless knight. Aye, auld Trent hated ma guts. He wanted me tae leave, but was frightened tae make me for he was scared o' me."

The powerful hands on his knees tensed and relaxed.

"Man, man, why stay on in all this hate and madness?" cried Hamish.

"It suited me. I'm a canny man. Money disnae grow on trees and we had the flat here for free. You know what they say about us Scots."

"The trouble with you mean Scots," said Hamish angrily, "is that you claim it as a national virtue, which gives the other ninety-nine generous per cent o' the population a bad reputation. I wass sorry for you when I heard about the trick Trent played on ye, but you're just as bad as your master ever was, in my opinion."

"Aye, but your opinion doesnae matter, laddie. It's that cheil, Blair, that's running the investigation. I ken you. You're nothing but the village copper frae Lochdubh and a damned crofter as well."

Hamish left with a decided desire to find Jimmy Gaskell guilty. He made his way down to the kitchen. Melissa was sitting at the table eating sandwiches and Towser was lying beside an empty bowl on the floor, asleep again.

"I was looking for some scraps for Towser," said Melissa. "I could only find a little bit of cold meat because I didn't want to annoy Enrico by taking anything bigger. But he came down after the reading of the will, asked what I was doing and when I told him, he gave Towser a pound of liver. How did it go?"

"Jeffrey and Jan, Paul and the Trent sisters are all going to be verra, verra rich. Enrico and Maria and the outdoor staff all get generous legacies. Charles Trent gets nothing."

"Oh, that's wicked," said Melissa. "Poor Charles. Surely the others will give him something."

"I'll be verra surprised if they do," said Hamish, pouring himself a cup of coffee and sitting down beside her at the table. "Don't you want to congratulate Paul?"

"No, I don't feel like it," said Melissa. "I just want to go home."

"Stick it out," urged Hamish. "Oh, here's Anderson."

Detective Jimmy Anderson wandered into the kitchen. "Anything to drink down here, Hamish?" he asked. "I went into the drawing-room where they've got the drinks, but the new millionaires told me to get lost."

"I'll ask Enrico," said Melissa. "He's in his quarters."

"Leave him," said Anderson. He rummaged through cupboards and found a bottle of cooking sherry and poured himself a large glass before sitting down at the table with them.

"Ah, that's better," he sighed, after taking a great swig.

"Rough time with Titchy?" asked Hamish sympathetically.

"Rough! That little lady knows more swear-words than the whole of Her Majesty's armed forces put together. She comes tripping in, batting her eyelashes at Blair and oozing sex. He rips into her. She takes a deep breath and bingo! Out goes Marilyn Monroe, in comes Lady Macbeth."

"What other reports did you get?" asked Hamish.

Anderson looked pointedly at Melissa. "Never mind her," said Hamish. "I'll get you some Scotch."

"You're on. But how?"

"Wait." Hamish went up to the drawing-room. There were bottles stacked on a trolley in the corner. He picked one up after the other while everyone watched him nervously. Then he seized a bottle of malt whisky, said, "Aha! Fingerprints," and marched out of the room with it.

"You're a genius," breathed Anderson, tossing back the remains of his sherry and filling the glass up with whisky. "Right, let me see. Charles, the adopted son. Can't find any adoption papers in the house. Cheerful layabout, popular, loads of girl-friends, usually of the upper-crust sort, until he met Titchy. One job after another. He always leaves, though. Bored. Doesn't get fired.

"Jeffrey Trent. Running into financial trouble. Wife of his eats money. Best address, best gowns, best jewels, latest in Jaguar cars, his is up here, hers down in London. So Jeffrey needed money badly.

"Angela and Betty Trent. Old maids. In their fifties, both. Angela the older. Live together. Had fairly generous allowance from Pops. Nothing there, except women at the menopause can go weird. Didn't like their dad and made no secret of it.

"Paul Sinclair." He looked at Melissa. "Are you ready for this?"

"Go on," said Melissa quietly. "I don't care any more."

"Okay. Bright boy. First in physics at Cambridge. Good worker. Clean habits. One nasty scene at his Cambridge college, Pembroke. Got drunk at college dinner and punched someone who called him a swot. Engaged to a girl student, Anita Blume. She dumped him. Broke down the door of her college room and wrecked the place, tossing the furniture around and screaming. In danger of being sent down but survived the scandal because brilliant student. Nothing else."

"Paul *violent*?" Melissa looked amazed. "You should see him when he's working at the atomic research station. Mild-mannered, serious, polite."

"Well, maybe mild-mannered Paul Sinclair jumped intae a phone booth and emerged as ... Supermurderer. Ta-ra!" cried Anderson, waving his whisky glass.

"Paul? Oh, no. No, he couldn't have," said Melissa, looking sick again.

"Run along, lassie," said Hamish. "I think you could do with a lie-down. Or get a book and go somewhere quiet by yourself."

Anderson grinned at Hamish after Melissa had left. "Are we getting a bit soft about Miss Punk Head?"

"No, but I think she's a decent girl."

"Aren't they all," said Anderson gloomily.

"What's the pathologist's report?" asked Hamish.

"Stabbed through the heart with great force. Sometime after dinner. Since he was seen alive at eleven o'clock and there was a body on the floor o' Titchy's room at midnight, then it stands to reason he was killed sometime during that hour."

"But is he sure of that?" asked Hamish. "We'd best have a look for that dummy, the one that was used before to frighten Titchy. Someone could have used it first and then dragged the dead body along later."

"That someone would need to be crazy. What if

Titchy had screamed the place down when she saw the dummy, just like before?"

"Yes," said Hamish thoughtfully. "But I think we are looking for someone crazy."

Melissa came back into the kitchen. She looked at Hamish. "Titchy wants to see you," she said.

Now what? thought Hamish. He asked Melissa to look after Towser. "Where is Titchy?"

"In the bedroom, Charles's bedroom."

Chapter Five

I wish I loved the Human Race;
I wish I loved its silly face;
I wish I liked the way it walks;
I wish I liked the way it talks;
And when I'm introduced to one
I wish I thought What Jolly Fun!

— Sir Walter A. Raleigh

"I feel I can talk to you," said Titchy Gold to Hamish Macbeth.

"What about?" asked Hamish cautiously. Titchy was sitting in a chair by the window of the bedroom she shared with Charles. Hamish had learned from the police report on Titchy that she was actually thirty-five. She certainly did not look it. Her skin was smooth and unlined and fresh. Her eyes, however, when her guard was down, held an odd mixture of cynicism and coldness. Again he found himself dis-

liking her but could not figure out why. It was not
that she had killed her father. Only Titchy knew what
dreadful cruelty she had had to put up with until
driven to that desperate resort.

With a sudden flash of intuition, he realized that it
was because Titchy did not like anyone: one of those
rare creatures who have a bottomless loathing for
their fellow man or woman. He was surprised she had
thrown such a fit of hysterics over the first trick played
on her and over the headless knight, particularly the
headless knight. Being an actress, she must be used to
stage effects. Perhaps it was because she threw scenes
as easy as breathing, or perhaps she was unbalanced.

"I just want to make sure I can walk out of here
tomorrow without that fat detective trying to stop
me," said Titchy.

"You've made a statement," said Hamish. "If the
police want you, they can visit you in London. But
why tell me?"

"Because I am not telling anyone else," said
Titchy. "I want to get away from here and forget I
ever knew any of them. Charles will fuss and fret and
say I'm dumping him because he's not coming into
any money."

"And would that be true?" asked Hamish.

"Of course. I've got my future to think of. If I married Charles, I'd end up working for the rest of my
life to support him and I'm not the maternal type.
Mind you, there's always dear Jeffrey."

"He's married."

"For the moment," said Titchy cynically. "Haven't you noticed the way he looks at that wife of his? He'll get rid of her now, I bet. Yes, Jeffrey might be an idea."

"You'd better go easy," said Hamish. "It is my belief that the murderer is in this house."

"And it could be Brother Jeffrey? Don't you believe it, copper. That sort only dreams of violence."

There was a noise from the corridor outside. Hamish ran to the door and whipped it open. No one was there.

"I think someone was listening at the door," he said slowly.

"Probably that Spaniard," said Titchy. "He gives me the creeps. He's always scuttling around, watching everybody. But do me a favour, and don't tell your superiors I'm leaving."

"Well..." Hamish looked at her. "I'll chust pretend you havnae spoken to me. But the results of the fingerprints should be through any time now. Don't you want to find who cut up your dresses?"

"Phone me in London and tell me. Whoever did it will get a bill from me. Send the clothes on to me." She scribbled down an address in Hammersmith and handed it to him. "Blair's got that, but I'd rather hear from you. You can't get fingerprints off clothes anyway, can you?"

"It's amazing what they can get fingerprints off these days," said Hamish. "How are you leaving?"

"I'll phone a taxi company in Inverness to come up and get me in the morning and take me to the airport."

"All that business about you and Charles Trent having a lovers' conversation in the snow on the night of the murder. It iss my belief, Miss Gold, that you told him you were leaving him. Then after the murder, when it seemed he might become rich after all, you decided between you not to tell anyone about breaking off the engagement, for that might lead them to think Charles had killed the old man to keep you."

"Think what you like," said Titchy indifferently.

Hamish rose to go but hesitated in the doorway. "If I was you, Miss Gold," he said, "I would chust leave quietly. Don't try to stir up any trouble."

She grinned but did not answer.

Hamish went back downstairs to the kitchen and collected Towser. "Where are you going?" asked Melissa.

"Down to the village again," said Hamish.

"Can I...can I come with you?"

"Not this time," said Hamish. "Blair's waiting for the result of those fingerprints and he'll want you all here."

After he had gone, Enrico and Maria came in and began making preparations for lunch. Melissa went up to the drawing-room. She looked ruefully down at her stained fingers, wishing she had washed them. They had all been fingerprinted earlier in the day.

Paul was having a low-voiced conversation with

his mother. Jeffrey Trent was standing by the fire-place, watching them. Betty was sitting knitting something in magenta wool, the needles clicking and flashing in the light. Her sister Angela was reading a newspaper.

Then the door opened and Detective Harry MacNab stood there. He looked across at Angela. "Miss Trent," he said, "you're to come to the library right away."

It was almost as if she had been expecting the summons. She calmly put down the newspaper, stood up, squared her shoulders and marched to the door.

She was not gone long when Titchy Gold appeared. Melissa blinked. Titchy was "in character." She was made up and dressed like the floozie she portrayed on television. She was wearing a short scarlet wool dress and she looked as if she had been poured into it. Her dyed blonde hair was once more dressed in her favourite Marilyn Monroe style. Her face was cleverly made up.

She went straight to Jeffrey. "Well," she said huskily, leaning one elbow on the mantelpiece and smiling up at him, "how does it feel to be a millionaire?"

Jeffrey's thin grey face broke into a smile. "Great," he said.

"Jeffrey!" Jan's scandalized voice sounded from the other side of the room.

Neither of them paid Jan the slightest attention. "And what are you going to do with it, you old money-bags?" said Titchy, twisting a coy finger in Jeffrey's buttonhole.

"I tell you what I'm going to do with it." Jeffrey's voice was loud and precise. "I am going off to lie on the beach somewhere and never, ever do a stroke of work again."

"Taking anyone with you?"

"No," said Jeffrey cheerfully.

Jan approached the pair, her thin hands clenched into fists. "Jeffrey, you appear to have forgotten that your brother has just been murdered. Do stop talking rubbish."

"But I'm not talking rubbish, my precious," said Jeffrey. "I am leaving you, Jan. I am going as far away from you as I can possibly get. It will do you good to try to support yourself for the first time in your greedy life, although I suppose you'll batten on that wimp of a son of yours."

One minute Paul was sitting with his head down. The next he had leaped across the room and seized Jeffrey by the throat. "No," screamed Jan. "Paul, don't—"

Paul released his stepfather and stood panting. Melissa felt shaken and sick. But Titchy appeared delighted. She linked her arm in Paul's. "Well, well, tiger cat," she cooed. "Why don't we go out for a walk," Paul shook his head in a bewildered way as if to clear it. His glasses were askew and he straightened them with a shaking hand and then went meekly off with Titchy.

"Where's Charles?" asked Betty Trent.

Jeffrey and Jan were staring at each other. "I don't know," said Melissa nervously. "I think I'll just go and—"

"Don't ever humiliate me like that again," said Jan.

"I won't be round to do it," said Jeffrey cheerfully. "I'm leaving you. I'm leaving Britain."

"You can't. I'll sue you."

Jeffrey suddenly looked years younger. "You'll never find me...ever," he said happily. "I may even take young Titchy with me."

"You forget, Miss Gold is engaged to Charles," remarked Betty Trent.

Jan rounded on her. "You don't think that little tart is going to marry Charles now that he hasn't any money. How incredibly stupid."

Betty folded up her knitting and stowed it away in a large cretonne work-bag. She looked at Jeffrey. "You're quite right to leave her," she said. "I have always considered your marriage a disaster."

Melissa ran out of the room and collected her jacket and headed down to the village. She did not want to join the others for lunch. There was no sign of Paul or Titchy outside.

The weather had made one of its rapid Sutherland changes. It was mild and balmy, the sun was shining, and the air was full of the sound of running water as the snow melted from the hill and mountains. A stream ran beside the road, gurgling and chuckling, peat-brown and flashing with gold lights. Before the entrance to the village was a humpbacked bridge. Everything seemed to shimmer and dance in the clear light. Melissa walked on, ignoring the crowd of reporters who were pursuing her with badgering questions. The only way she knew how to cope with them was to pretend they weren't there. Fortunately for her, just as she reached the bridge, one of them shouted that he had just seen Titchy Gold walking in the grounds and they all scampered off, leaving her alone.

In the main street, she saw a café and headed for it, hoping it was not one of the ones which opened only in the tourist season.

But as soon as she approached it, she saw through the glass of the front window the tall figure of Hamish Macbeth. She opened the door and went in.

"I thought you were investigating something," she said accusingly.

"I wanted to get away on my own and think for a bit," said Hamish amiably.

A waitress approached and asked Melissa what she wanted. Melissa realized she was very hungry.

"Have you anything local?" asked Melissa hopefully.

The waitress recited in a sing-song voice, "Pie and chips; sausage, bacon and chips; ham, egg and chips; haggis and chips; hamburger and chips."

Melissa ordered ham, egg and chips. "Beans is extra," said the waitress.

"No beans."

"Is that yer own hair, lassie?"

"Yes," said Melissa stiffly.

"How did yiz do it?"

Melissa glared.

"She really wants to know," said Hamish sotto voce.

"Oh, in that case, I bleached it first and then dyed it pink. It's a dye called Flamingo."

"My, it's right pretty. Flamingo, did ye say? Maybe my man'll be able tae get it in Inverness."

"You're changing fashion in the Highlands," said Hamish. "It is nice now you've washed all the gel out of it. But won't it be awfy difficult when your roots start showing?"

"Yes, it will. But I'll just dye it back to my normal colour. Oh, there was the most awful scene in the drawing-room." She told him what had happened.

"You'd better get that boy-friend of yours away from her, for a start. She's out to make trouble."

"I don't want to have anything more to do with Paul," said Melissa. "But the thing that puzzles me is that Titchy was Charles's fiancée when he didn't have money or the prospect of it. She must have been fond of him."

"I think she was fond of his looks," said Hamish. "He is a verra good-looking young man and she was often photographed with him. I think that was the attraction. Also, perhaps after sleeping her way into show business, she found having a good-looking lover a refreshing change. Where was he when all this was going on?"

"I don't know. Nobody appears to have seen him today."

"They might find out who it was who cut up Titchy's frocks."

"Oh, I forgot to tell you," said Melissa. "Before I left, Blair sent for Angela. So *she* might have have been the one."

"Ah. Here's your food. I'd better leave you."

"Can't you wait? I won't be long."

"I cannae be seen too often in the company of a murder suspect," said Hamish deliberately.

Melissa gave him a wounded look.

"Think about it," said Hamish. "As far as Blair is concerned, you're engaged to Paul. Paul might have known about the will, so you might have known about the will and you could have planned the whole thing between you."

Melissa's large grey eyes filled with tears. "You're horrid." she said shakily.

He relented. "Look, I'm trying to frighten you into being on your guard. Don't trust any of them."

"If Angela cut up the dresses," said Melissa, anxious to keep him longer, "does that mean she might have committed the murder?"

"I think it might mean she thought Titchy was being too successful in engaging the auld man's affections and wanted to put a spoke in the wheel."

"Poor Angela," murmured Melissa. "Blair will be giving her a dreadful time."

Hamish rose to go. "I think Blair will find out that Miss Angela Trent is not easily bullied."

Detective Chief Inspector Blair was glaring at Angela. "I do not think you realize the seriousness of the matter," he said in carefully enunciated English. "One of thae...those...frocks had bugle beads on the trim and those beads carried bits of your fingerprints."

"Have I protested?" boomed Angela. "Have I said otherwise? Yes, I admit I sliced the seams of those frocks. My motive was simple. Titchy Gold was flirting disgustingly with my father. I was afraid he would leave her something in his will. I knew she would suspect him of being the culprit, which she did. Quite clever, really. If Miss Gold feels like pressing charges, I shall settle out of court, and handsomely too. So pooh to you."

Blair crouched forward over the desk and snarled, "Your father was murdered. In my opinion, a woman who could play a trick like that could murder her ain father."

"Oh, really? Well, you do not strike me as being a very intelligent man. In fact, while you are wasting your breath and bullying me, there is a murderer in this house."

Angela suddenly raised a handkerchief to her lips, as if she realized for the first time that there *was* actually a murderer lurking about.

Blair plodded on, taking Angela back over the evening leading up to the murder, checking everything against the statement she had previously made.

At last he growled at her to keep herself in readiness for further questioning and Angela lumbered off.

"Strong woman, that," said Jimmy Anderson. "She could ha' done it."

"I'll just keep on until one o' them breaks," said Blair. "Fetch Charles Trent in again. He's the one who would have expected to inherit."

It took some time before Charles could be found. Harry MacNab at last ran him to earth in the games room, where he was trying to play a game of table tennis with himself by hitting the ball and darting around to the other side of the table to try to return his own serve.

Blair looked up as Charles Trent was ushered into the room. The young man looked a trifle pale but carried himself easily.

"Well now," began Blair, "that will must have come as a shock to you."

"Yes," said Charles Trent. "Of course it did. I mean, if he had left it to a home for retired parrots or something, it would have been less than a shock. But to leave something to everyone *except* me, well, that was a bit of a blow."

"So what will you do?"

Charles smiled ruefully. "Work, work, work, I suppose. Pity, I was looking forward to a life of ease."

"Is there any way you or anyone else could have known what was in that will?" asked Blair.

"Don't think so," said Charles. "We were all strung up before the reading of the will. If you think I killed him because I thought I was getting something, you're way off beam. You have to hate to commit a murder like that. *He* hated *me*. *I* didn't like *him*. But that's another thing entirely."

Blair doggedly continued to question him for another hour.

Charles left feeling depressed but he brightened at the sight of Titchy. She was standing in the hall with her back to him, talking to Enrico.

"I want you to move my stuff out of Mr. Charles's room," he heard Titchy say. Enrico inclined his head and moved quietly off.

"What's this?" demanded Charles. "Ditching me, Titchy?"

She flushed when she saw him. "Well, it's not quite the thing, Charles dear, us sharing a room when we're not married. Angela and Betty are so stuffy."

Charles looked down at her. "I repeat: Are you ditching me, Titchy?"

She looked at him defiantly. "Why not? You're a waste of time."

His eyes went quite blank and he stood very still. "I could make you very, very sorry," he said quietly.

The drawing-room door opened. Betty Trent stood there. Behind her were the others: Paul, his mother,

Jeffrey, Angela, and Melissa, who had just joined them. They were sitting in various frozen attitudes looking out at the couple, revealed through the door held open by Betty.

"Are you threatening me?" screeched Titchy.

"Think about it," said Charles coolly. "Just think what I could do to you."

He walked out through the front door into the melting snow.

Titchy shrugged and laughed. Numbly Betty stood aside to let her into the drawing-room. Everyone stared at her silently.

"Don't let me spoil your fun," said Titchy. "What were you all talking about?"

"They were talking about you," said Melissa suddenly. "Angela was asking Jeffrey if he really meant to go off with you and Paul said if you did, he would murder you."

"Melissa!" exclaimed Paul in a hurt voice.

Melissa rounded on him. "You asked for that," she said fiercely. "You brought me up here and landed me in the middle of a murder and yet all you've done since we were brought back from Inverness is run to your mother or flirt with that tart."

"My, my," said Titchy, who seemed to be enjoying herself immensely. "Jealousy will get you nowhere, pet, nor will pink hair, for that matter. So old-fashioned. Dead seventies, that."

"Jealous…of *you*?" raged Melissa. "I don't care

who Paul runs after. He's nothing to me. You're all sick!"

Hamish Macbeth wondered what was going on as Melissa erupted from the drawing-room, but he had decided he had better tell Blair about Jim Gaskell, the gamekeeper, and so he went on into the library.

Blair swore when he heard about the trick played on the gamekeeper. "There's damp suspects comin' oot o' the woodwork," he groaned. "Anderson, fetch that gamekeeper in here. And Macbeth, arnae you neglecting the duties o' your parish? There's no need for you here fur the rest o' the day."

"If it hadn't been for me," said Hamish stiffly, "you'd never haff heard about the gamekeeper."

"Aye, aye, laddie. Jist piss off and take that mongrel wi' ye. You should know better than to take your pet on a murder case."

"I told you before," said Hamish. "This is a trained police dog."

"If thon thing's a trained police dog, then I'm Lassie," hooted Blair. "Off wi' ye."

Hamish muttered under his breath as he and Towser scrambled into the police Land Rover. It was already dark, the north of Scotland seeing very little daylight during the winter. As he approached Lochdubh, he thought of calling on Priscilla and then changed his mind. She had called him a moocher. She would think he had only called at the hotel to cadge a free drink. He drove on towards the police

station. At the end of the waterfront, the Lochdubh
Hotel stood dark and empty. It was usually closed for
the winter, but rumour had it that it was being put up
for sale because the competition from Tommel Castle
was killing off trade.

He parked the car and let himself into his kitchen,
noticing as he switched on the light that frost was
forming on the inside of the window and that last
night's dirty dishes were still in the sink.

He lit the kitchen stove and cooked some kidneys
for Towser and then walked up and down rubbing his
hands, waiting for the room to heat up.

There was a tentative knock at the kitchen door.
He thought it was probably the minister's wife, Mrs.
Wellington, who expected payment in fresh eggs
from Hamish's hens for walking Towser.

But it was Priscilla who stood there, and she was
holding a foil-covered dish.

"Truce," she said. "I brought you dinner. Vension
casserole. It only needs to be heated up."

"Come in," said Hamish eagerly. "I'm sorry I
snapped at you, Priscilla, but Blair drives me mad
and I wass hungry and . . . and it's grand to see you."

"That's more like it." Priscilla put the casserole into the oven and sat down at the kitchen table.
She slipped off her wool coat, which crackled with
electricity from the frosty air. "Turned cold again,"
she said. "Damn winter. I'm sick of it. I would like to
go and lie in the sun on a beach somewhere."

"Like Jeffrey Trent," said Hamish. He sat down as well and told her what had happened that day, ending up with, "I don't like the way Titchy Gold is going on. But then I don't like Titchy."

"Why?" asked Priscilla.

"I don't know. She's such a mixture. One minute she's as hard as nails, the next she's playing the vamp...and neither of those characters ties in with the one which was sick with fright over the appearance of that headless knight."

"I think I know why. A lot of theatrical people are very superstitious, Hamish. Do you think she did the murder and then calmly went to bed with her lover?"

He shook his head. "I don't know," he muttered. "But when I see her, I see death."

"But to get the body in the wardrobe in the first place, you would need someone very strong...or two people," pointed out Priscilla.

"Aye. They could all have done it, to my mind. Of course, the whole setting is unnatural, Priscilla. There's that over-heated house, the ghastly noisy carpets and furnishings, all in the shadow of the mountain...so I'm looking at all these people through a distorting glass."

"What about Jan Trent? Instead of getting the servants to clean up to protect her son, she could have been protecting herself. She loves money, you said."

"Aye," agreed Hamish. "Then there's the daughters, Angela and Betty. Odd couple. One of them couldn't have done it, but two...although Angela Trent's a hefty woman. Mind you, both had a generous allowance from the old man while he was living. If they did not know what was in the will, why kill him and kill the goose that was laying the golden eggs?"

"When there are millions to be inherited," said Priscilla, "even a generous allowance can begin to seem like a pittance." She went to the oven and took out the casserole and served the contents deftly onto a plate. We're like an old married couple after all the passion has long died away, thought Hamish, at first privately amused, and then, for some reason he could not fathom, angry. He had a sudden childish desire to push the food away and say it was not very good. He then wondered uneasily if he was coming down with some sort of virus. He always got tetchy just before a bout of the flu.

"Anyway, I'm out of the case," said Hamish. "Blair has ordered me back. I don't see much hope of solving it long-range."

"I know Angela Trent very slightly," said Priscilla. "Daddy took me to Arrat House on a visit when I was a child. I could always go over there to offer my sympathies and tell you what's going on."

Hamish brightened. "I wouldn't mind a fresh eye on the case," he said eagerly. "Also, you could keep an eye on Melissa. She's a nice little thing and I worry about her."

"Oh, really? The one with the pink hair?"

"Yes. It's an odd thing, but the pink hair suits her. She's got nice eyes."

"And Miss Pink Punk wouldn't hurt a fly?" demanded Priscilla sarcastically.

"In my opinion, no," said Hamish, his mind too deep in the case to notice the sarcasm.

Priscilla got up and put on her coat with brisk nervous movements. "I'm off, Hamish. I'll think about going over to Arrat House, but there's a lot to do at the hotel."

Hamish looked at her in hurt surprise. "But I thought ye said ye were going!"

"Well, we'll see." Priscilla went out and banged the kitchen door behind her with unnecessary force.

A sort of torpor seemed to have descended over Arrat House the next day. The hard frost of the night before had given way to a thin weeping drizzle driven in on an Atlantic gale. Blair was restless and tired. He had been commuting between Strathbane and Arrat, leaving late at night and arriving early the next morning. Soon he would need to take final statements and let them all go. He could charge Jan Trent and Enrico with interfering with the evidence, but he was perfectly sure the hellish Spaniard would promptly send that tape to his superior.

He settled down in the library and rustled through his notes. Surely he should be concentrating on the one likely suspect and that was Titchy Gold. She was a murderess and therefore the one person who was likely to kill again. He looked up at Anderson. "Get that actress in here again," he said gruffly, "and let's see if we can get mair oot o' her."

Anderson walked out. Titchy was not with the others, who were sitting morosely in the drawing-room. He asked if anyone had seen her.

"She's probably still asleep," said Betty, knitting ferociously, the light from a lamp above her head shining on the busy needles.

Anderson went down to the kitchen and asked Enrico to take him up to Titchy's room.

"I put her in another of the guest bedrooms," said Enrico as he led the way up the stairs. "She no longer wanted to share a room with Mr. Charles."

He pushed open a door. Both men looked inside. Titchy was lying in bed on her side, her blonde hair tumbled over the pillow.

"You'd better wake her up," said Anderson.

Enrico called, "Miss Gold!"

The figure in the bed did not move.

The manservant approached the bed. He took a tissue from a box beside the bed and then shook Titchy's bare shoulder with one tissue-covered hand.

Anderson was amused. "I'd heard butlers and folk like that werenae supposed to touch the mistress's bare flesh when waking her in the morning, but this is the first time I've ever seen anyone do it."

Enrico straightened up and turned to face the detective. "I think Miss Gold is dead," he remarked.

"Whit? She cannae be, man." Anderson strode to the bed and jerked down the covers. He felt Titchy's body and then uttered an exclamation. The actress was cold and rigid.

"Get Blair," snapped Anderson. "Man, man, this is terrible."

While he waited for Blair, he bent over the body again. He saw no signs of violence. There was a cup and saucer beside the bed. He bent over the cup and sniffed it. It smelt of chocolate.

Blair came crashing in, his eyes bulging out of his head.

"Tell me she's had a heart attack," he roared, "but jist don't tell me there's been another murder."

An hour later, Superintendent Peter Daviot gazed bleakly around the assembled police and detectives in the library. He looked like a younger version of Jeffrey Trent.

"So," he said, "a murder was committed under your noses. Were any police on duty last night?"

"Two patrolling outside last night and two mair this morning," said Blair. "There's nae accommodation here, sir, and—"

Daviot held up his hand for silence. "Now the preliminary opinion of the pathologist is that she died from a possible overdose of sleeping pills. Who in this house takes sleeping pills? I just hope it turns out she did it herself."

Anderson opened his notebook. "Angela and Betty Trent," he said, "and Mr. Jeffrey Trent. A bottle of some stuff called Dormadon is missing from Jeffrey's bathroom cabinet, but the servants say the Trents never locked their bedroom door and so anyone could have got in."

"Have you interviewed any of them yet?" demanded Daviot.

"No," oiled Blair. "The minute we heard you were coming, we decided tae wait."

"Right," said Daviot. "We'd better see Charles Trent first. I gather he was heard threatening Miss Gold, or so Mr. Jeffrey Trent obligingly told me as I arrived." He paused. "Where's Hamish Macbeth?" he asked.

"He's back at Lochdubh," muttered Blair.

"Whatever for? He's covering this area for Sergeant MacGregor. He knows the locals. It may not be an inside murder. Get him back over here immediately."

Anderson raised a hand to hide a grin as Blair reluctantly picked up the phone and dialled Lochdubh police station and then in strained, polite tones asked Hamish Macbeth to return to Arrat House and briefed him on the death of Titchy Gold.

A man from the forensic team popped his head

round the door. "No fingerprints on that cup," he said cheerfully.

"Well, that's that," said Daviot gloomily. "You are not going to persuade me that a suicide wiped that cup clean. Get Charles Trent."

Charles Trent looked strained and shaken. "Sit down," said the superintendent. "We have reason to believe that your fiancée did not take her own life. Now you were heard to threaten her yesterday. You said something like, 'I could make you very, very sorry.' And when Miss Gold asked if you were threatening her, you replied, 'Just think what I could do to you,' or words to that effect. What did you mean?"

Charles put a hand up to his brow. "I was miffed because she was dumping me, and quite heartlessly, too. I wanted to get back at her. I meant that I could sell my story about our relationship to one of the sleazier tabloids, that's all."

"Did you go to her bedroom last night?"

He shook his head. "There didn't seem to be any point. It's all my fault, in a way. She was happy enough with me before I roused her expectations about that damned will. She got greedy, that's all. But why would anyone kill her?"

"Did she upset anyone apart from you?" asked Daviot.

"I believe she was making a play for old Jeffrey, and that upset his wife. You'd better ask her."

"We will." Charles was then questioned exhaustively about his movements the day and night before. He seemed to gain composure rather than lose it as the questioning went on.

At last Daviot sent him away and asked for Enrico to be brought in.

Had anyone, he asked the Spaniard, used the kitchen the night before? Enrico said that Miss Angela had come down about eleven o'clock in the evening for a glass of hot milk. Earlier, Mrs. Jeffrey Trent had come in to make herbal tea, Charles Trent had wanted a sandwich, and Melissa Clarke had asked for a flask of tea for her room.

Blair interrupted, his voice loaded with sarcasm. "Whit's a' this? Don't these grand folks just ring the bell and ask fur ye to bring whatever it is they want upstairs?"

Enrico looked mildly amused. "It is not the Middle Ages," he said in his precise English. "Maria and I had served dinner. It is generally understood that we are off duty after that."

"Quite, quite," said Daviot hurriedly. "It is believed the sleeping pills, if that's what they were, were put into a cup of hot chocolate. Where is the chocolate kept?"

"In the large cupboard in the pantry off the kitchen with the other dry groceries."

"And was the carton of drinking chocolate still there this morning?"

"Yes, members of the forensic team took it away."

Daviot then questioned him all over again about what time he had gone to bed and if he had heard anyone moving about the kitchen. Enrico said that he had gone to bed about midnight and that he and his wife would not remark particularly if they heard any sounds from the kitchen. They would assume one of the guests had come down for a late drink or snack. No, he could not remember any particular sounds. He had gone to sleep almost immediately.

Daviot glanced through the file he had already read on the road up. "Let us go back to the first murder. I see here that you removed the body of Mr. Trent and laid it out in the games room and then cleaned the bedroom upstairs. Can you tell me in your own words why you did that?"

Enrico's eyes flicked briefly to Blair. "It was understood at the beginning that Mr. Trent had been the victim of one of his own practical jokes. My wife and I did what we thought was fitting."

Daviot swung round to Blair. "Would you say that was correct as far as you could judge from your investigations?"

"Aye," said Blair and mopped his forehead. He was dreading the arrival of Hamish Macbeth. What if Hamish told Daviot about Mrs. Trent's paying the servants to clean up? Daviot would wonder why they had not been charged.

Daviot questioned Enrico further and then dismissed him.

"Now," said Daviot, "I would like an independent witness." He studied a list of names in front of him. "Let's have the Clarke girl in."

Melissa felt she was living in a nightmare. She clung to the hope that it would turn out that Titchy had murdered old Mr. Trent and then had taken her own life. She was vaguely relieved that the questioning was started by Blair's superior and not Blair.

"Now," said Daviot, "take your time. We need you to tell us what went on yesterday."

In a shaking voice, Melissa said, nothing in particular. All she wanted to do was to get away from this room-ful of policemen. But Daviot probed on and on, question after question, until Melissa found she was telling him everything—about Titchy's flirting with Jeffrey, about Jeffrey's saying he was leaving his wife, about Paul's attacking Jeffrey, every little thing until she felt weak and exhausted and near to tears.

When she had been dismissed, Daviot frowned down at his notes. "We seem to be getting more suspects by the minute instead of less. Oh, well, we'll have Jan Trent in next."

Jan was wearing a severe tweed suit with a white blouse and sensible brogues. She slid into the chair opposite Daviot, folded her skeletal hands on her lap, and waited.

"Now, Mrs. Trent," began Daviot, "your husband told you publicly that he was leaving you. Is that not true?"

Jan gave a slight shrug. "He said something like that. But Jeffrey has been extremely overwrought."

"He also said he might take Titchy Gold with him. He was attacked by your son."

"Jeffrey was behaving outrageously. I fear the murder of his brother has turned his mind. My poor Paul has been in an understandable state of nervous tension." Her voice sharpened. "I will not have you bullying him."

Daviot questioned her closely about her movements the previous night and then took her back through her movements on the night of the murder of Mr. Trent. Throughout the interview, Jan seemed to come under increasing strain. She pleated a handkerchief between her long fingers, then smoothed it out on her knee, and then began to pleat it all over again.

The superintendent watched her closely. He became sure that she might have committed murder in the hope of getting money through her husband.

After he had finished with her, he decided to interview the dead man's daughters.

Betty was the first. She seemed strained and shocked. Her dumpy figure was encased in correct mourning and her eyes were red. "I am not sorry about the death of that silly girl," she said. "In fact, I'm glad. She was, she must have been unstable. It stands to reason. She killed Dad and then took her own life."

"That would be a very comfortable solution," said

Daviot. "Unfortunately, the cup which contained, we think, sleeping pills, was wiped clean. I do not think anyone bent on committing suicide would do that."

Betty burst into tears and then, between sobs, she said incoherently that the police were fools and simply letting the investigation drag on and on out of sheer sadism.

Daviot gave up trying to question her further and she was led from the room.

She was replaced by her sister Angela, who appeared made of sterner stuff. Angela said roundly that she had thought about the murders and was sure they had been done by some maniac from the village. "There's a lot of inbreeding in these Highland villages," she said. "Mark my words, while you are wasting your time questioning us, there is some drooling homicidal maniac loose in Arrat."

She then grumpily described what she had been doing the night before, movements which Daviot noticed were as vague as everyone else's. No one so far could put an exact time on where they had been last evening or when they had gone down to the kitchen.

Paul Sinclair was next. His face was white and there were purple shadows under his eyes, but he told them his movements in a quiet, measured voice. "Now let's go back to yesterday afternoon," said Daviot. "You attacked your stepfather when he said he was leaving your mother, did you not?"

"The bastard was jeering at her," said Paul. "She's my mother, for God's sake! You wouldn't expect me to sit there and say nothing."

"You have a record of outbursts of rage," said Daviot quietly. "It is possible, you know, that you could have killed Titchy Gold because your stepfather was insulting your mother by suggesting he might take Titchy with him when he left her."

Paul looked at him wearily. "You can't pin that one on me. Poisoning is hardly the action of someone given to outbursts of rage. Nor did I kill old Mr. Trent. I had no interest in his money. I am going to sign most of it over to my mother."

"Had you already discussed such an eventuality with her—in the event of Mr. Trent's death?"

"No, of course not," snapped Paul. "I did not expect Mr. Andrew Trent to die. He was as fit as a flea when I arrived. I did not expect to inherit anything. Why should I? I thought it would all go to Charles. I only came up to this hell-hole to please my mother."

He was questioned about his movements for half an hour before he was allowed to go.

Jeffrey Trent was summoned next. Of all the people Daviot had interviewed, Jeffrey seemed the least affected; in fact, he looked positively cheerful. He said he had had no intention of going off with Titchy Gold but had merely said so in order to get revenge on his wife.

For what?

For years of complaint and humiliation, for the years she had bled him like a leech, said Jeffrey. No, he had not liked his brother Andrew. Yes, he had simply come to Arrat House in the hope of getting something in his brother's will. He answered all questions in a dry, precise manner but underneath it all ran a current of amusement that Daviot found highly irritating.

"Well, that's that for now," said Daviot when he had finished questioning Jeffrey. "We will sit and go over what we have heard while we wait for forensic reports and the pathologist's report."

The door of the library opened and a tall, gangly figure wandered in.

"Hamish!" said the superintendent. "Sit down, lad, while we discuss this case."

Blair shifted uneasily. Somehow, the superintendent had a habit of calling Hamish Macbeth by his first name when he was displeased with him—Blair. What if Daviot were to go back to the laying out of the body and what if Hamish Macbeth were to tell him the truth?

Chapter Six

It is a riddle wrapped in a mystery inside an enigma.

—Sir Winston Churchill

Priscilla Halburton-Smythe had some difficulty getting into the grounds of Arrat House. The narrow road leading to it was crowded with reporters, photographers and television crews. Satellite dishes like giant mushrooms glinted palely in the grey light. Ignoring the questions shouted at her by reporters, she rolled down the window and explained to one of the policemen on guard that she was a friend of the family. This was not true, but Priscilla could hardly explain she had arrived for the sole purpose of helping P.C. Hamish Macbeth in his inquiries.

At last she was through the crowd of press and inside the gates. Enrico answered the door. Priscilla asked for the Misses Trent and gave her name. Enrico knew the name of every landowner from Arrat to the coast as well as any Highlander and so ushered her into the drawing-room. They were all gathered together, all the suspects.

"You won't remember me," said Priscilla, advancing on Angela. "I came here as a child. I am Priscilla Halburton-Smythe. I came to offer my condolences. The death of your father is a terrible tragedy. Is there anything I can do to help?"

"Decent of you to call," said Angela, "but there's nothing to do at the moment. We haven't had the hearing at the procurator fiscal's yet and we can't even plan the funeral. Sit down. Enrico, fetch Miss Halburton-Smythe a drink or something."

"Too early, and call me Priscilla."

"I'd better introduce everyone," said Angela. "I feel I should say, enter first murderer and this is the second murderer." She gave a shrill laugh.

"Control yourself," snapped her sister. "I am Betty Trent. The tall young man over by the window is Paul Sinclair and the girl with pink hair is Melissa Clarke. To your left is Jeffrey Trent, our uncle; and to your right, his wife Jan. Charles is over there, by the fire. Now, have you heard the latest news?"

Priscilla shook her head.

"That actress has been found murdered."

"Titchy Gold!"

"The same."

"How was she murdered?"

Betty's composure suddenly broke and she stared

in an anguished way at Priscilla, opening and shutting her mouth.

"Sit down, Betty," said Jeffrey. "I'll explain. Titchy Gold was found dead in bed. A cup beside the bed was found to have been wiped clean of prints. A bottle of my sleeping pills has gone missing. We are waiting for the pathologist's report and can only pray it turns out to be natural causes. If it hadn't been for someone wiping that cup clean, then we might have supposed she murdered my brother and then took her own life."

"And I suppose the police suspect one of you," said Priscilla. There was a shocked silence. But why are we so shocked? thought Melissa. We've known all along one of us did it.

"I think it was that Spaniard, Enrico," said Angela at last.

"Why?" asked Priscilla. Melissa suddenly experienced a fierce stab of resentment against this cool and beautiful blonde who asked questions with the impersonal incisiveness of a policeman.

"Why?" echoed Angela. "'Cos he's greedy and he's got money in the will. Oh, stop snivelling, Betty. You're getting on my nerves. No guts, that's your problem."

"And you're an insensitive moron," howled Betty.

Charles's voice cut across the row. "Now look what you've done, Priscilla," he said. "We've all endured a morning of questioning and then you come along and pour salt on all the wounds."

Priscilla flushed. "I am sorry," she said. She felt like an amateur. Hamish Macbeth would never have been so abrupt. She began to talk to Angela of her memories of her visit to Arrat House. Angela said she thought she had some old photographs taken during that visit and brought out an album. Priscilla bent over it. Yes, there she was herself, about age six, and there were Angela and Betty with their father, who was roaring with laughter about something. The small boy was recognizable as Charles. He was clinging on to the skirts of both sisters and looking over his shoulder with a look of horror on his face.

"What frightened you?" Priscilla asked Charles. He crossed the room and bent over the album. "Oh, that day. That was the man hanging in the tree."

"One of Dad's jokes," explained Angela bitterly. "He had one of the gamekeepers pretend to be a hanged man. Frightened poor little Charles out of his wits."

"And me," said Priscilla, suddenly remembering that day clearly. She had felt sorry for Charles. Her furious parents had promptly taken her away and she had wondered for a short time afterwards what it was like to have to live with a parent who played such infernal tricks. Betty, who had recovered, said she had heard about Tommel Castle being turned into an hotel and asked how the business was going. Priscilla talked away while all the time she stored up impressions of the people gathered in the drawing-room to tell Hamish. Charles had a sort of bland ease of manner over an undercurrent of nervousness. Jan was silent, strained and fidgeting the whole time. Betty was listening to the tales of running the hotel as if they were the most interesting stories she had ever heard. Angela was sitting four-square, her hands on her knees, staring into space. Melissa and Paul were having a low-voiced conversation at the window. Jeffrey was the only one who seemed at all at ease, as if the macabre goings-on at Arrat House had nothing to do with him.

Enrico reappeared and said that Charles was wanted in the library and the others exchanged looks as he walked out.

Priscilla rose to go. "I gather you are all being kept indoors," she said to Angela. "Can I get you anything from the village?"

Angela said there was nothing she needed but Betty brightened. "Perhaps you could get me some more wool in this shade from Mrs. Tallisker's at the end of the village. It's no use asking Maria. She always comes back with the wrong colour."

Happy to have an excuse to return to Arrat House, Priscilla went out into the hall. Melissa followed her, with Paul close behind. "Could you smuggle us out past the press in your car?" asked Melissa.

"It might upset the police," said Priscilla. "They'll probably want to interview you all over again."

"Just for a short time," begged Melissa. "I feel

I'll go mad if I don't get out of here. Paul, too." Paul blinked at Priscilla myopically. Melissa was now feeling quite motherly and protective towards Paul. He had apologized to her that morning for his behaviour. He had begged her to help him get through this ordeal.

What would Hamish expect her to do? wondered Priscilla. Perhaps she might gain some useful information from Melissa and Paul.

She made up her mind. "All right, then. But you'd both better crouch down in the back seat until I get past the press. Where do you want to go?"

"There's a little café-restaurant in the village," said Melissa eagerly. She saw Enrico hovering in the shadows of the hall and lowered her voice. "Where is your car?"

"It's a white Volvo, round the right-hand side of the house," whispered Priscilla.

"We'll go out the back way and meet you," said Melissa urgently.

Soon Priscilla was driving carefully down to the village, with Melissa and Paul crouched down under travelling rugs in the back seat.

"Here we are," she called over her shoulder as she parked outside the café. "Won't the gentlemen of the press find you?"

"Not in a café," said Melissa, popping up from under the rug. "They all go to The Crofter, the pub further along."

"I'll go and get Betty's wool," said Priscilla, "and then I'll join you both."

"Nice girl," said Melissa as she entered the café with Paul.

"Yes," agreed Paul, "and very beautiful."

Melissa did not like that comment much. "Now, Paul," she began, after they had ordered cups of coffee, "you must try to pull yourself together. The killing of Titchy can have nothing to do with you or me. We've only got to survive another day or two of questioning and then they'll need to let us go."

He drew patterns on top of the wax table-cloth with the edge of his teaspoon. "What if Mother did it?" he said.

Melissa took a deep breath. She privately thought Jan was capable of murder, but she said, "Of course she didn't do it! Why should she? You know, Paul, your mother is quite capable of looking after herself. I wouldn't run mad and give her all your money, but certainly enough to make her independent. I know: Tell her to go off on a cruise. That way you would be free of her for a bit and get a chance to settle down."

Paul blinked at her mistily and took her hand. "That's what I like about you, Melissa, your strength."

Melissa gently disengaged her hand. She knew she was not a strong person. A strong person was like Hamish Macbeth. She wondered what it would be like to be a policeman's wife. She wondered why he had never married. She dimly realized Paul was speaking.

"I've always been dominated by Mother, Melissa, and the time has come to really break free. I can't do it right away while she's upset over this break-up with Jeffrey. But once she's settled, I'll see less of her. That cruise is a good idea."

They were joined by Priscilla. "I managed to get that wool," she said cheerfully. "I'll need to take you back soon or Blair will start howling and cursing."

"Do you know Detective Chief Inspector Blair?" asked Melissa.

"Yes, I have met him. We had a murder in Lochdubh last year."

"Lochdubh? Oh, you must know Hamish."

A slight tinge of frost crept into Priscilla's eyes. "Yes, he is a friend of mine."

"Oh." Melissa looked at her doubtfully and then her face cleared. Beautiful rich girls like Priscilla did not have anything to do with village constables. "Ready to go?" asked Priscilla, who had suddenly decided that it would be a waste of time to keep them out longer by interrogating them.

She drove back to Arrat House thinking perhaps it was as well Hamish was off the case. Melissa was a nice little thing, but too silly and susceptible. She parked the car at the side of the house. Melissa and Paul climbed out. And then ambling around the side of the house came Hamish Macbeth. Melissa let out a glad cry and ran straight into his arms, babbling about the second murder and about how frightened she had been, but now that he was back everything was all right, while Priscilla and Paul looked bleakly on.

Hamish disengaged himself quickly. "You'd best get indoors, Melissa, before Blair finds you were out of the house. A word with you, Priscilla."

Melissa stood and stared as Hamish and Priscilla walked off together. They were both tall and looked at ease with each other.

"Have you been flirting with Melissa?" Priscilla was asking.

"I wass chust being my usual charming self," said Hamish. "I am back on the case. The rest are having lunch but I wanted a bit of fresh air."

"Where is Towser?"

"Being looked after by Mrs. Wellington. Priscilla, there's been another murder, and right under the noses of the police, too. I've mair to worry about than one spoilt mongrel. What did you find out?"

"Not much. Betty asked me to pick up some wool for her from the village and Melissa and Paul begged a lift. It's a difficult business. There they all were and one of them a possible murderer. But with the atmosphere of Arrat House and the horrible furnishings, anyone looks like a murderer. Enrico is creepy. He hangs about listening, have you noticed? Paul Sinclair is a drip, in my opinion. He seems, at a guess, to be using that Melissa to try to get free from his mother. Hamish! I've suddenly thought, who was Mr. Sinclair? I mean, who was Paul's father? There might be insanity in the family, something like that."

"There's a point," said Hamish. "The rain's started again. We're getting awfy wet, Priscilla."

"There's a summer-house thing over by the woods. We'll go there."

They walked into a rather damp and dilapidated summer house and sat down together. "I was reading an article about genes and heredity," said Priscilla.

"That's all verra well," put in Hamish, "but I've never noticed murder running in families."

"No, but insanity does."

"Maybe," he said slowly. "I'll ask Anderson. He's been ferreting into everyone's past."

"I can do it easier than that," said Priscilla eagerly. "I'll just ask Paul."

"What? If his father was bonkers?"

"No, silly. I'll ask if his father is still alive, and if so, where, and if not, what did he die of."

He gave her a slow smile. "My, my," he mocked. "Quite the detective. And here's me thinking you didnae want tae come to Arrat House."

"I found I had less work at the hotel than I thought," said Priscilla primly.

Hamish clasped his hands behind his head and looked meditatively at the ceiling. "Aye," he said dreamily, "that Melissa iss a nice wee lassie."

"Hamish Macbeth. Unless you are seriously interested, leave her alone. She's upset, young and far from home, and highly susceptible."

Hamish grinned. "I wass only teasing," he said, but Priscilla had already risen to her feet. "One of us had better do some work," she said sharply, and walked out of the summer house.

Melissa, watching from the drawing-room window, saw her approach, saw the long easy strides, the immaculate hair, the well-worn but well-cut tweeds, the air of assurance and clasped her arms about her body and shivered. It was always the same. She would find some man to dream about, some man to hope for, and then just when she began to imagine she had a chance, some female appeared over the horizon and took the man away. She gave a little sigh. The Melissas of this world always had to settle for second best. "Don't look so gloomy," came Paul's voice from behind her. "We'll soon be out of this nightmare."

The drawing-room door opened and Priscilla came in, holding the parcel of wool she had bought for Betty. "Where is everyone?" she asked.

"They're all in the dining-room," said Melissa. "Neither of us felt like eating anything."

"I'll go and give this to Betty," said Priscilla. She hesitated in the doorway. "Is your father still alive?" she asked Paul.

He blinked at her in surprise.

"No," he said curtly. "He died shortly after Mother divorced him."

"I am sorry," said Priscilla. "What did he die of?"

"A broken heart," snapped Paul. "So go and report that to your policeman friend."

"There's no need for you to get so worked up," said Melissa when Priscilla had left. "And what makes you think she is spying for Hamish?"

"Because she goes off with friend Hamish and then comes back for the express purpose of trying to find out about my father. It was all Jeffrey's fault. He took Mother away."

"Try not to get so upset." Melissa took his arm. "Maybe we should get some food after all." She smiled up at him. "Don't worry. I'll take care of you."

His eyes filled with tears and he took off his glasses and scrubbed at them with his handkerchief. "Thank God you're here with me," he said in a choked voice. "Oh, Melissa, will you marry me?"

She stared back at him. Somewhere at the back of her brain a tiny warning voice was crying that Paul wanted a substitute mother, that her remark, "I'll take care of you," had sparked the proposal. But there were louder voices and bright images. He was a tolerably personable young man with a good job. He was a millionaire. She would have a diamond ring. Mum would be ever so pleased. White satin. Who would be her bridesmaid? Church. Bells ringing. Modern home. Shiny kitchen. Herself in apron. Had a good day, darling?

"Yes," said Melissa.

*   *   *

They were drinking coffee when Priscilla entered the dining-room. Betty accepted the wool with a cry of delight and begged Priscilla to join them. "Did you have a terrible time getting past the press?" asked Charles.

"Not really," replied Priscilla. "I kept the car windows closed and let the police guide me through."

"It shouldn't be allowed," said Angela. "Ghouls and vultures."

"Understandable," put in Jeffrey. "I mean, Titchy Gold and people like her cultivate publicity. You can't turn it off like a tap just because she's dead."

"The press have descended on us in hordes," said Charles evenly, "not because of Titchy's publicity hunting but because two murders have been committed in this house."

"Yes, yes, dear," said Betty hurriedly. "But let's not talk about it."

"As you wish," said Charles, "but not talking about it isn't going to make the problem go away."

"It's because each one of us is a suspect that we're all so frightened and nervous," said Jan, "and that's ridiculous. Andrew Trent tormented the villagers and the outside staff as well. This house is never locked, neither are the bedrooms. Anyone could have come in from outside."

Charles glanced out of the window. "You may have your wish," he said. "That gamekeeper, Jim

Gaskell, is being marched in for interrogation. The police lunchbreak is obviously over."

Enrico, who had just brought in a fresh pot of coffee, said smoothly, "Perhaps the police now know that Jim Gaskell had more reason than most to want Mr. Trent dead."

"How? Why?" demanded several voices.

Enrico told them about the trick played on the gamekeeper.

"There you are!" said Jan triumphantly when he had finished.

Charles shrugged. "Let's hope he keeps the police busy for the rest of the day. I'm tired of questions."

"Don't you want to find out who did it?" demanded Jeffrey.

"Of course I do," said Charles. "My fiancée has been murdered. But I wish they would start looking in other directions. They keep going on at me. They should be looking for some homicidal maniac."

The door opened and Paul and Melissa came in. Jan looked at her son sharply. "I'm glad someone's happy," she declared. "Don't tell me that idiot Blair has actually found the murderer."

Paul took Melissa's hand in his. "We're to be married, Mother. Melissa and I are engaged."

"That's all I needed," said Jan. Everyone else murmured their congratulations. Priscilla looked at Melissa and thought, she's not in love with him. After all this is over, she might regret it.

*   *   *

While Jim Gaskell was being interrogated, the preliminary autopsy report on Titchy Gold came through.
She had died from an overdose of sleeping pills. Furthermore, the forensic experts had already discovered
traces of sleeping pills in the dregs of the chocolate.

The gamekeeper listened impassively and then said,
"So what are you wasting time questioning me for? I
didnae kill the lassie, nor had I any reason for doing so."

Daviot sighed and dismissed him but told him to
be available for more questioning.

"Was that dummy found?" Hamish asked suddenly.
"I mean, the first joke that was played on Titchy was
with a dummy."

"Yes, we found it," said MacNab. "It was down in
a store-room next to the games room along with a
bunch o' other tricks."

"What did they all really think of Andrew Trent?"
said Hamish, half to himself.

"Whit does that matter?" demanded Blair.

"Whoever killed him hated him, really hated
him," said Hamish. "If we solve the first murder,
we'll know the answer to the second. Although they
may not be connected."

"Never say that," groaned Daviot. "But you have
a point. Let's have 'em all back, one after the other."

Jan Trent was the first to be asked to reply to the
simple question, "What did you think of Andrew
Trent?"

She looked at them, slightly goggle-eyed with amazement. "What did I...? Well, not much. Just a silly old man. Jeffrey didn't like his brother much and did not see much of him, which meant I didn't see much of him either."

"What did your first husband do?" asked Hamish.

"He was a bank manager."

"What did he die of?"

"A heart attack," snapped Jan. "What has all this got to do with...?"

"Quite," said Daviot, throwing a curious glance at Hamish. "Let us revert to the original question. What were your feelings towards Mr. Andrew Trent?"

She sat silent for a few moments and then said, "Impatience, mild dislike, that's all."

When she had gone, Hamish asked, "Where did her husband die?"

"John Sinclair died in a nursing home in Ealing," said Anderson, consulting a sheet of notes.

"An ordinary nursing home?"

"I think so. Why?"

"I just wondered whether it might have specialized in mental patients—whether there's any insanity that might have been passed on to the son."

"I'll check," said Anderson and picked up the phone.

Charles Trent was next. Asked what he had thought of his adopted father, he said in a puzzled way, "Well, not much. Irritating old cove. I mean, I was sent away to boarding-school early on and left there as much as possible. It suited me. I didn't like holidays at home. Then, after a bit, some of the boys used to invite me to their homes for the holidays and I liked that. I wished he'd been more like a real, ordinary father, you know. But I've always been pretty popular, lots of friends and all that, and he did pay up for a good education. I kept away from him as much as possible. It suited both of us."

"And you didn't hate him?" asked Daviot, thinking again what a singularly beautiful young man Charles Trent was.

"Not enough to murder him, if that's what you mean," said Charles.

He had no sooner left the library than Anderson said cheerfully, "You might hae something, Hamish. John Sinclair was as nutty as a fruit-cake. He did die of a heart attack. But the nursing home takes mental patients. He got out one night and was found running around the grounds in the middle of winter without a stitch on. They had to put him in a strait-jacket, and while he was fighting and struggling, he had the heart attack that killed him."

"Right," said Daviot. "Let's see what Paul Sinclair has to say to that."

Hamish thought Paul Sinclair was thoroughly prepared for this line of questioning. Priscilla must already have asked questions about his father and that had alerted him.

He said quietly that his father had been perfectly sane until the divorce, which had turned his mind. "And do you blame your mother for your father's death?" asked Daviot.

Cold anger blazed momentarily in Paul's eyes but he had himself well in check. "Of course not. I blame Jeffrey Trent. He took my mother away. He told her that if she married him I would have the best schools, the best of everything. It was all his fault."

Daviot leaned forward. "And what did you think of Andrew Trent?"

"I couldn't stand him," said Paul. "Filthy old fool and his disgusting jokes."

Daviot's voice was cold and even. "Did you murder him?"

Paul snorted with contempt. "No. I was getting away. I had planned to leave in the morning with Melissa. We all hated him. I'm the only one who's honest about it."

Betty Trent was next. She looked shocked when asked to tell them her feelings towards her father. "Well, how odd of you. I mean, he was my father. I loved him. His jokes were very tiresome, I admit, and Angela and I would not have come to visit him had we not believed him to be dying. You are very insensitive, Superintendent. What a horrible question to ask a recently bereaved daughter! It is possible to love a parent without liking him, you know."

They did not get much farther with Angela, although she was more forthright than Betty. She said she and Betty had dreaded coming to Arrat House because of the practical jokes. They had not lived with their father for over twenty years. When they were both in their early thirties, Andrew Trent had had a house in Perth but had moved north when Arrat House and the land came up for sale. Although not Scottish, he had always wanted to be the laird, said Angela. She and Betty had persuaded him to let them go to London and live there. Hamish Macbeth said quietly, "Neither you nor your sister ever married. Did your father have a hand in that?"

"I suppose he did in a way," said Angela, "but if you think either of us killed him because of that, you're mistaken. Oh, I know people say, 'The poor Trent sisters, they were quite good-looking in their youth and could have got married had it not been for their father.' Sometimes I would like to believe that myself. He did play his awful tricks on any fellow we brought home. But the fact is," she said, her voice becoming harsh, "no one ever loved either of us enough."

There was a long silence in the room while Angela fought for composure. By God, Hamish Macbeth thought, if the auld scunner were alive this day, I would be tempted to kill him myself!

After Angela, Jeffrey Trent came as something of a relief. He was dry and brisk. No, he had not liked his brother much, but as he had had little to do with him, he had not entertained any strong feelings against him. At present, he felt quite fond of his late brother because of the inheritance. It had given him the freedom he craved.

"Both Paul and Mrs. Trent say you took her away from her first husband, John Sinclair, thereby causing the man to have a mental breakdown," said Hamish.

"Pah," snorted Jeffrey. "She threw herself at me. And men like John Sinclair don't turn raving mad because a stick insect like Jan has left them. They've been raving mad all along."

Were they all as dreadful as they sounded, thought Hamish, or was the brooding presence of the two murders making them seem worse than they were?

He almost regretted having been called back from Lochdubh. He felt he could get a clearer perspective if he could get away from Arrat House and think. He glanced out of the windows of the library. The rain had stopped and a thin pale sunlight was filtering through the glass. Charles Trent and Priscilla were walking up and down outside, talking. He wondered what they were talking about.

"I wish I could get away from here," Charles was saying. He had accompanied Priscilla outside after she had said her good-byes. Sunlight was sparkling on the slushy snow and the air held a hint of warmth. "It's so far from everything. I never felt at home here and it wasn't entirely because of Father and his dislike of me or his hellish jokes. Sutherland is a foreign country, a different race of people, a different way of thinking. Outside that overheated house, I was always aware of the vastness of moorland and mountain. I love the city, the lights, the theatres, the bars, the noise and bustle. Sometimes when you walk out into the country here at night, the silence is so complete it hurts your ears. The land is so old, so very old, thin earth on top of antique rock." He shivered. "Why am I telling you all this?"

"Because I'm a stranger," said Priscilla gently. "Because I'm not a murder suspect. Did you really love Titchy?"

He gave a rueful laugh. "If you had asked me that twenty-four hours ago, I would have said yes and meant it. That's what's so awful. She's dead, murdered, gone forever. I didn't really know her at all. That detective, the foxy one, Anderson, he told me that she had been sentenced for killing her own father. Maybe I'm a shallow person. I take everyone at face value. She was blonde and beautiful and everyone envied me, or I thought they did. We were always in the newspapers and I liked that. I don't think about anything very deeply when I'm in the city, but up here . . . well, there's nothing to hide behind, no trappings of civilization. Then who would murder Titchy? Not one of us, surely. They keep hinting that I hated my father. They can't seem to understand that I didn't have any strong feelings about him whatsoever. If I'd been unhappy at school, it might have been different. Can you understand that?"

"Yes, I think so," said Priscilla cautiously. "When are the police going to let you go?"

"Soon, or we'll have a team of lawyers up here making sure they do. Doing anything tonight?"

Priscilla looked at him in surprise. "Are you asking me out?"

"Yes, why not? Drive off somewhere for a bit of dinner."

"Well..."

"Priscilla, might I hae a word with you?" The quiet voice of Hamish Macbeth sounded behind them.

Priscilla found to her annoyance that she was blushing like a schoolgirl caught out in some misdemeanour. "Yes, certainly," she said. "Charles, would you excuse us?"

"Let me know about dinner," he said and loped off.

"What is it, Hamish?" asked Priscilla.

"I haff to go back to Lochdubh tonight and I was hoping for a chance to discuss the case wi' ye. Of course, if you prefer to go jauntering off with a murder suspect..."

"Don't be silly, Hamish. I haven't even had time to think. All right, then, I'll pick up some food for us on the road home and I'll be waiting for you at the police station about seven, say."

"Fine." Hamish's hazel eyes swivelled to the

entrance of the house where Charles was lounging, watching them curiously.

"So I'll deal with my admirer, if you deal with yours," said Priscilla.

"Who?"

"Melissa, just coming around the corner of the house."

Priscilla walked off as Melissa strolled up to Hamish. "Heard the news?" demanded Melissa.

"What news?"

"Paul and I are engaged to be married."

"Why?"

"Why?" echoed Melissa. "What an odd thing to say. Aren't you supposed to offer the lady your felicitations?"

"I suppose. You don't look like a woman in love."

"What does a woman in love look like, Hamish?"

"She looks happy. You don't look happy, Melissa."

"How in the hell am I supposed to look happy when I'm living in a place where two murders have been committed?" Melissa turned on her heel and strode off. Could Hamish...might Hamish...be a little jealous? Melissa's steps faltered as her heart yearned towards that thought, but then she strode on as common sense took over, or what she decided was common sense. The Melissas of this world, she told herself sternly, were not destined to fall in love and get married. The lucky Melissas of this world settled for a nice man with money. *A man given to outbursts of rage*, taunted a voice in her head, and she shook it impatiently, as if to get rid of that mocking voice, and concentrated on a happy vision of a white wedding instead.

Priscilla collected the key to the police station from Mrs. Wellington, listened politely to the minister's wife's complaints that she could not go on looking after "that mongrel," collected Towser and then let herself into Hamish's narrow kitchen and began preparations for the meal. Why on earth didn't Hamish Macbeth get himself a gas cooker? she thought, not for the first time, as she lit the black iron stove. Hamish's large brood of little brothers and sisters over at Rogart were doing well, and so was his parents' croft. They did not make demands on his money any longer, that she knew, but the years of necessary thrift had bitten deep into Hamish, she supposed. She made a simple meal of grilled lamb chops, baked potatoes and a large salad. It was almost ready by the time Hamish arrived.

How intimidating she looks, thought Hamish, as he paused in the kitchen doorway and removed his peaked cap. She had changed into a plain wool dress the colour of spring leaves and was wearing green high-heeled shoes of the same colour. Not a hair of her smooth blonde head was out of place. A dumpy little woman in an apron with mussed hair would have looked much more at home in his dingy kitchen.

"Tired?" she asked.

"A bit," said Hamish, sinking down into a chair and patting Towser. "Rather, my brain's tired. I cannae get the *feel* of anyone. One minute I think it's your beau, Charles, the next I think it's Paul. Oh, Melissa's to marry Paul. I wonder if I can talk her out of it."

"The only way you're going to talk her out of it is by offering yourself as a substitute," said Priscilla, putting the food on the table. "I brought mineral water to drink. I thought we would need all our wits about us."

"Aye, that's grand. What was Charles Trent talking about?"

"He was quite interesting," said Priscilla. "The redcurrant jelly is by your elbow." She told him all that Charles had said.

"He's probably being very clever and hoping you'll repeat all this to me."

"Could be. But I didn't get that impression. I think he's usually a carefree sort of chap who's been rocked by all this murder and mayhem. I think, when it's all over, he's about the only one who will come out of this untouched by it."

"No sane person could come away from two murders and remain untouched by it," said Hamish. "And talking about insanity, I think Paul Sinclair's got a bad temper, that's all. I don't really believe much in all this business of insanity running in families. People so often go mad with alcohol or drugs or Alzheimer's disease or things like that."

Priscilla looked stubborn. "I think you should concentrate on Paul Sinclair. With a father like that—"

She stopped and stared at Hamish.

"What's the matter?" he asked. "You look as if you've been struck by lightning."

"Who were Charles Trent's real parents?"

"We couldn't find any adoption papers. Besides, what does it matter? You've got a bee in your bonnet about this hereditary thing."

"But wouldn't it be interesting?"

"I would hardly know where to start," said Hamish. "Wait a bit. Perth. That's where old Trent must have been when he adopted the boy. But I can hardly rush off to Perth tomorrow. I'll be expected back at Arrat House first thing."

"I could phone up Strathbane and say you were sick. They won't really mind. The place is crawling with detectives and policemen and forensic teams. I'd take you to Perth myself."

"We'll probably only discover that his old neighbours, if they're still alive, hated him as much as everyone else," said Hamish gloomily. "On the other hand, I don't like the thought of my mind getting bogged down in the atmosphere of Arrat House. One day wouldn't matter, I suppose."

"I'll phone now," said Priscilla.

Blair listened to her explanation that Hamish Macbeth was suffering from a virus infection.

"And is this his mother speaking?" he asked with heavy sarcasm.

"You know very well who is speaking," said Priscilla coldly. "If you are unable to take this message, put me through to Superintendent Peter Daviot."

"No, no," said Blair hurriedly. "Jist ma wee joke." He knew Daviot, a snob, would hit the roof if he thought Priscilla had been insulted.

Priscilla returned to the kitchen. "Well, that's that," she said cheerfully.

"It still seems a bit daft," said Hamish. "What are you hoping to find? That Charles Trent's parents were maniacs?"

"Something like that," said Priscilla, unruffled. "At least it would be a start."

Chapter Seven

If your lips would keep from slips,
Five things observe with care.
To whom you speak; of whom you speak;
And how, and when, and where.

—William Edward Norris

For the first time in years the bedroom doors at Arrat House were locked at night. Jan and Jeffrey Trent still shared the same bedroom, lying without touching, the air between their bodies twanging with hate. Not particularly an unusual state of affairs in a marriage but adding to the tense and frightening atmosphere of Arrat House. The wind had got up, that famous Sutherland wind, howling and baying and shrieking, taking away any feeling of security engendered by thick walls, thick carpet and central heating, raising dormant fears in civilized minds of the days when Thor, the god and protector of warriors and peasants, rode the heavens. The old gods and demons of Sutherland had taken over, tearing through the countryside over the cowering heads of petty men.

And women.

Melissa Clarke lay awake. One particularly furious blast of wind boomed in the old chimneys and shrieked across the roof.

She switched on the light. They would never return here, she thought. They would go on honeymoon to Italy or France.

The wind dropped for a few seconds and she heard a soft shuffling noise from the corridor outside her room. Then the wind returned in force. She lay rigid, staring at the door.

As she looked, the handle of the door began to turn slowly. This was not a horror movie, she told herself sternly. Police were patrolling outside and a policeman was on guard in the hall downstairs. But she was unable to move.

The doorknob turned again. She looked wildly around. There must be some sort of bell to ring the servants. Yes, there was one over by the fireplace. But she was paralysed with fear. There was no way she could get out of bed and walk over to that bell. And then she noticed that the doorknob was still again, unmoving, the light from the lamp beside her bed winking on the polished brass.

She lay there for a long time, listening to the heaving, shrieking and roaring of the wind, and then, quite suddenly, she fell asleep.

When she awoke early in the morning, the wind had dropped. She hoisted herself up on one elbow and looked in a dazed way at the door, wondering if she had imagined it all. And suddenly the room was filled with hellish, mocking laughter. Her terror grew as she realized it was not mechanical laughter from one of old Mr. Trent's machines. It was from the world of dark nightmare. It was from the sulphurous pit where the demons dwelled. Sobbing with fear, but somewhat emboldened this time by daylight, she found strength to leap from the bed and run to that bell and lean on it, ringing and ringing the bell, sweat pouring down her body. She heard the sound of footsteps running up the stairs and then a hammering at the door. Whimpering with relief, she went to it and turned the key and flung it open. Enrico was there, with a policeman behind him.

"I'm haunted," gasped Melissa. "That laughter."

Both men stood and listened. Nothing.

"I heard it," wailed Melissa.

And suddenly, the hellish laughter started again.

Enrico went to the fireplace and peered up the chimney.

"Jackdaws," he said in disgust. "And I took a nest out of this chimney only last year."

"You must be a townee," said the policeman. Melissa sank down on the edge of the bed. "It's dreadful," she said. "Are you sure it's only jackdaws?"

"Yes," said the policeman. "Right nasty noise they make."

"I'm sorry to have troubled you, but I was so frightened. You see, someone tried the handle of my door last night."

"What time was this?" asked the policeman.

"About two o'clock this morning."

"You should have rung the bell then," he said severely.

Melissa put a hand up to her head. "I was so frightened, I couldn't move. The only reason I found courage to ring that bell this morning was because it was daylight."

Paul Sinclair appeared in the doorway. "What's going on, Melissa?"

Melissa told him about the turning doorknob and the jackdaws.

Paul blushed. "Actually, I tried your door last night. I wanted to talk to you."

"At two in the morning?" asked the policeman suspiciously.

"I couldn't sleep," said Paul defiantly, "and we *are* engaged to be married."

Enrico straightened up from the fireplace. "I can prepare you an early breakfast if you would like."

"Oh, that would be nice," said Melissa, feeling a little surge of power, despite her recent distress, at being able to give orders to a servant. "Some scrambled eggs and coffee, Enrico, and what would you like, darling?"

"Just toast and coffee," said Paul. "I'll see you downstairs, Melissa. Won't be long."

After they had all gone, Melissa began to wash and dress. They would have servants, she thought. Perhaps a couple to live in. Not British. A couple of foreigners. Of course, only the terribly rich could afford servants, but Paul would be very rich if he did not give all that money away to his mother. Melissa's soft lips moulded themselves into a hard line. Why should he? Why should Jan have everything? They could have a flat in town and perhaps a nice old farmhouse in the country. That *would* be nice. Chintz and beams, and put the car away, Costas, and tell Juanita to bring in the drinks for our guests. Yes, all that should be hers. And clothes like those worn by Priscilla. Expensive, subtle clothes. Real materials, silk and fine jersey wool and chiffon velvet. Best seats at the theatre, a box, even. First nights. Little parties. Villa in the south of France. Send the servants ahead with the luggage and tell them to get things ready. Plane to Marseilles and Costas waiting with the white Rolls Royce to run them along the coast to where their summer home was perched on a thyme-scented hill above the blue of the Mediterranean. Parents at the wedding...

The dream began to splinter. Mum and Dad would need to wear nice clothes and be very, very quiet so that no one could hear their accents. And smelly old

Auntie Vera was definitely not coming. Hairbrush poised above her head, Melissa thought, why get married in church at all? Simple service in a registry office, brief visit home to Mum. Surprise, surprise. Got married. Isn't it fun? So no embarrassment of workingclass parents and relatives at the wedding. Yes, that was the way to do it. Now to get Paul to keep that money. Why should both of us work? If he loved her, he would surely rather please her than his mother. Give the old trout something, but not all.

Dreams of wealth were so rosy that they kept the fear engendered by the murders at bay and so the more highly coloured they became in Melissa's mind.

She went down the stairs determined to start work on Paul right away.

Jeffrey Trent wandered into his nieces' bedroom later that morning. "What a storm last night!" he said. "I could hardly sleep."

Betty was sitting at the dressing-table unrolling old-fashioned steel curlers from her head. Angela was sitting up in bed, reading *The Times*.

"I slept through it all," said Betty to Jeffrey's reflection in the mirror. "Are you still set on leaving Jan?" she went on. "I mean, it does seem rather odd in someone of your age."

"Meaning I shall shortly die an unhappy man anyway? No, Betty, I plan to enjoy myself."

Angela put down the paper. "I've often wondered why you married Jan in the first place. I liked your first wife, Pauline. Very sweet."

"She was all right," said Jeffrey, "but a bit frigid, if you must know. That was the attraction about Jan. She hooked me into bed half an hour after she had first met me."

"Jeffrey!" Betty looked at him in distress.

"Well, it's the truth. Manipulating bitch that she was. Oh, it was a successful marriage right up until the money began to dry up. Now I'm going to get my revenge. It's a pity I can't talk Paul out of giving her any money."

"Talking about money," said Angela, "I do think it's awful that Charles hasn't got anything."

"I suppose we could give him some," said Betty. "What do you think, Jeffrey? I mean, we're going to have millions each, aren't we?"

"Yes, even after death duties. I think I'll give him something myself... and tell Jan."

Angela looked uncomfortable. "You mustn't be so spiteful. After all, you're getting your freedom. Leave the woman alone. Why so bitter?"

"You haven't been married," said Jeffrey, "so you don't know what it's like to be sucked dry of money. That parasite deserves every pain I can give her."

"Jeffrey is being quite horrible," said Jan to her son. "He seems determined to ruin me."

Paul pushed at the frame of his glasses with a nervous finger and looked owlishly at his mother. "You'd best get a divorce, and quickly," he said, "and then you'll be shot of him. Why are you still sharing the same bedroom? Enrico could find you another."

"I'm not going to let him off easily," said Jan. "I'm going to make him pay and pay."

"If he beetles off to South America, as he's threatening to do, you won't be able to get anything out of him. Don't worry. Haven't I promised to give you my share?"

Jan's eyes misted over with grateful tears. "You are the very best son any mother could have. What is it, Melissa? I didn't see you standing there."

"I just wanted a word with Paul," said Melissa.

Paul took her hand. "Go on," he said. "We're listening."

"In private, Paul."

Paul smiled at his mother and then went out with Melissa, who led him upstairs to her bedroom. She locked the door behind him. "Just so that we're not disturbed. The police have started their damned questions again."

"What do you want to talk to me about?" asked Paul.

"Well, it's about us. You've asked me to marry you and yet we've never made love or anything."

Paul blushed. "Plenty of time for that after we're married."

"But you might kiss me or something like that." Melissa gently took off his glasses.

Paul, who was a virgin, was not destined to remain so. If anyone had told him that a bare quarter of an hour after kissing Melissa he would be lying in bed naked with her, he would not have believed them. But that was how it happened. Quick, sharp, clumsy, but most satisfying. He felt marvellous. He felt ten feet tall.

"What do you say to a flat in town and a cottage in the country, somewhere near the research station, when we're married?" he realized Melissa was saying.

"Take a lot of money for that," he said sleepily.

Melissa took his hand and laid it on her breast. "But you'll have a lot of money," she pointed out.

He caressed her breast, marvelling at the smoothness of her skin. "Trouble is, I've promised Mother the lot."

"Now that's silly," cooed Melissa. "I mean, she doesn't need it all. A bit for her and the rest for us. That's fair. You wouldn't want to deprive our children of a good education.

"Children," said Melissa softly. "Lots and lots of them and we may as well start now."

She did a few ecstatic things to his body. Paul's last thought before another wave of red passion crashed over his head was that his mother was not going to be very pleased.

At last he fell asleep, wrapped in her arms. Awake,

Melissa stared at the ceiling and thought hard. It was not that she was mercenary, she told an imaginary Hamish Macbeth. It was just that if Paul was going to get all that money, why should she let him give it away? Like most women of low self-esteem, Melissa was like six characters in search of an author, always looking for a role to play to keep reality at bay. The new one was to be wife and mother. But *rich* wife and mother.

Hamish Macbeth and Priscilla were speeding down the A9 to Perth. "I feel a bit guilty about this," said Hamish. "It's like a holiday. It's like not having to go to school on exam day."

"We might find out something," said Priscilla. "Thank goodness, they haven't had the snow down here as bad as we did in Sutherland."

"I've never asked you," said Hamish curiously, "what you think of being stuck in Lochdubh all year round. I mean, you used to go off to London for most of the year."

"Oh, I like it. It suits me. It was a bit of a shock at first, I mean having to live permanently in an hotel. It's not as if we ever close down. But ever since Mr. Johnson took over as manager, things have been much easier. Daddy's had the architects in. We're going to build a gift shop next to the hotel and I'm going to run it. No tourist trash. I'm going to have all the best Scottish stuff I can find. After all, the sort of guests we have can afford to pay for the best. I can always go and stay with a friend in London if I feel I want a break from Sutherland."

"It was just what Charles Trent said started me thinking. I mean, your father's English."

"Never let him hear you say that," said Priscilla in mock horror. "He's ordered a kilt—evening dress. He says the guests will like it. What do you think of them all at Arrat House the further away you get from it?"

Hamish gave a groan. "They all seem quite ordinary. Now if old Mr. Trent had been alive and someone else had been killed, I would point to him and say, 'There's your murderer.' I mean, you have to be wrong in the head to want to go on playing awful jokes like that and know everyone hates you for it."

"I wonder if he did know," said Priscilla. "There's Blair Atholl Castle. Not far to go now. I mean, everyone toadied to him in a way. Look, no snow here at all and the sun is shining. Another world."

Hamish took out notes he had made on the case and studied them until Priscilla drove into Perth. "We'll start with the hospital," said Priscilla. "Have you got Charles Trent's date of birth?"

"Yes, he told Anderson it was November 5, 1964."

The main hospital had no record of a Charles Trent or in fact a Charles anything having been born at the right time. Adoption societies seemed to be housed in the larger towns like Aberdeen, Edinburgh and Glasgow.

"This is a waste of time," said Hamish. "All this way on a wild-goose chase."

"Let's have lunch," said Priscilla, "and find out what to do next."

"As long as I'm paying," said Hamish. Her remark about him being a moocher still rankled, though why this latest remark should rankle when previous ones had not he had not worked out—or did not want to work out.

"What about a burger then?" he asked.

"Don't insult me. I meant a proper lunch. Mr. Johnson said there was a good wine bar in the centre."

The wine bar turned out to be very good indeed, and to Priscilla's relief the prices were modest. Hamish began to enjoy himself. Perth, he thought, was a little gem of a town—good shops, good restaurants and the beauty of the River Tay sliding through its centre.

They were sitting over cups of excellent coffee when Priscilla called the waitress over and asked her if there were any hospitals on the outskirts of Perth, or maternity homes. "There's a wee cottage hospital on the road out to the west," said the waitress. "It's called the Jamieson Hospital. Blaimore Road."

"There you are," said Priscilla triumphantly. "We can try there."

"Before we do," said Hamish, "let's go to where

Andrew Trent used to live and see if any of the neighbours can remember him."

Andrew Trent's former home was on the outskirts of the town, a large brown sandstone double-fronted house, with a bleak gravelled stretch in front of it ornamented with dreary laurels in wooden tubs. A legend above the door proclaimed it to be the Dunromin Hotel. As they approached the main doors, they could see various geriatric guests peering at them from a front lounge window, like so many inquisitive tortoises.

The air inside had an institutional smell of Brown Windsor Soup, disinfectant and wax polish.

The girl at reception fetched the owner, who turned out to be an old lady of grim appearance. "Well, out with it!" she demanded. She jerked a gnarled thumb in the direction of the lounge. "Whit's that lot been complaining about now?"

"We are not here because of a complaint," began Priscilla.

"Just as well," said the owner. "They're never satisfied. Always phoning up their nieces or nephews or sons or daughters to say they're being cheated or getting poisoned or some such rubbish." Priscilla gathered Dunromin was one of those sad hotels which catered for permanent elderly residents cast off by their families, who did not want the indignities of the nursing home and so settled for the indignities of the cheap hotel instead.

"What we wanted to ask you, Mrs....?" said Hamish.

"*Miss* Trotter."

"What we wanted to ask you, Miss Trotter, was whether you bought this house from Andrew Trent, who used to live here in the early sixties."

"Aye, I did. And what's it to you, may I ask? I paid a fair price for it."

"Look," said Priscilla patiently, "Mr. Macbeth here is a policeman investigating the murder of Andrew Trent. Did you not read about the murder in the newspapers?"

Miss Trotter's eyes gleamed. "Oh, it was him, then. I thought it was someone else. That's a bit of luck. Mrs. Arthur at Ben Nevis next door is always bragging about how the chap that mugged old Mrs. Flint once stayed there. I'll have a murdered man. She'll be green with envy. Yes, that will put madam in her place. In fact, I'll just get my coat and run over there."

"Before you go," said Hamish, "did Mr. Trent have a baby in the house when you came to buy it?"

"Not that I can recall."

"What about the other neighbours?"

"You could try Mrs. Cumrie, two doors away on the right. She was here when I moved in."

Mrs. Cumrie was very old, wrinkled and frail, but with bright sharp eyes. Yes, she said, she remembered Andrew Trent and had not liked him one bit. No, he hadn't played any tricks on her. She had thought him a bully. He always seemed to be shouting and complaining about something or another. Yes, she remembered the baby. She did not know he had adopted it. She had assumed it belonged to some relative who was staying in the house. The baby had had a nanny, but she couldn't remember the woman's name or whether she had been a local.

"So that's that," said Hamish.

"Not yet," pointed out Priscilla. "We've still got the Jamieson Hospital."

Her spirits sank, however, when they arrived outside the hospital. It was small but new, certainly newer than thirty years.

They asked for the matron and put their request to her. She shook her head. "I would help you if I could," she said. "But the hospital was burnt down ten years ago and all the records were lost in the fire."

They gloomily thanked her and rose to go. They were just getting into the car when the matron appeared at the entrance and called them back.

"I've just had a thought," she said. "My mother was a midwife in Perth for years. She might be the one to help you. Even if she can't, she'd be right glad of some company. Wait a minute, and I'll write the address down for you."

"I suppose we'd better try everything since we're here," said Hamish as they drove off. "I'd clean forgotten about midwives. Charles Trent's mother could have had the baby at home."

The matron's mother was a Mrs. Macdonald. She lived in a small neat council house, new on the outside, but belonging to an older age on the inside where it was furnished with horsehair-stuffed chairs and bedecked with photographs in silver frames. Although very old, Mrs. Macdonald was a tiny, agile woman. She insisted they had tea and as soon as it was served began to hand them one photograph after another, telling them about deliveries long past and their difficulties. "I was a great amateur photographer in my day," said Mrs. Macdonald. "These were all taken with a box Brownie. Now that little laddie there is now Ballie Ferguson. He sometimes comes to see me, yes. You'll be having children of your own one day, Miss Halburton-Smythe, but I suppose you'll be going into the hospital. It's become fashionable again to have babies at home, though. Funny how the old ways come back."

"Mrs. Macdonald," said Hamish desperately, "I am a policeman, investigating the murder of a Mr. Andrew Trent. You may have read about it in the newspapers."

"And this one here," said Mrs. Macdonald, apparently deaf to his question, handing a photograph to Priscilla, "is Mary McCrumb. She calls herself Josie Duval now and runs a wee French restaurant in Glasgow. She never did like the name McCrumb. Pretty baby and an easy delivery."

"Andrew Trent," said Priscilla firmly. "A baby was born in Perth and he adopted it."

"And this is Jessie Beeton. Lovely wee dress, that. Nun's veiling. Cost a fortune."

Hamish signalled with his eyes that it was all hopeless.

They rose to go. "You must excuse us," said Priscilla. "Thank you for the splendid tea."

Mrs. Macdonald's childlike eyes showed disappointment. "I'll just see you out then," she said. "I talk too much, I know that, but I get lonely, although my daughter's a good girl and comes as much as she can. Watch the step there. What was you saying? Trent. Ah, yes, poor little Miss Trent."

Priscilla and Hamish, now both outside the front door, turned slowly, as though being pulled by wires. "What about poor little Miss Trent?" asked Hamish.

"I swore on the Bible not to say a word," said Mrs. Macdonald, "but that's when Mr. Trent was alive and you say he's dead now?"

"Yes, murdered, and you really must tell me what you know," said Hamish. "Promises, even ones made on the Bible, must be broken if you know something which will help the police in a murder investigation."

"Yes, yes, I suppose . . . Come back in."

"Let her tell the story in her own good time," Hamish muttered to Priscilla. "We'll get more out of her that way."

Priscilla marvelled at his patience, for they had to wait while another pot of tea was made and more scones produced.

"Well, let me see," she began. "The two Trent ladies lived in Perth. Miss Betty got into trouble. Miss Angela had taken up an interest in archaeology at that time and was off in foreign parts. Perth was a smaller town then but I never found out who the man was. Miss Betty would not say. Mr. Trent came to see me. A fine-looking man. He said that it was a dreadful scandal, and of course, it would have been if news of it had leaked out. Now what I tell you may make Mr. Trent sound a hard man, but forget what you've heard about the Swinging Sixties. For a woman of Miss Betty's standing, it was a scandal to have an illegitimate child. Mr. Trent said that Miss Betty would be kept indoors from the time she started to 'show.' He said he would move out of Perth after the birth, take the baby with him, and bring it up as his own son or daughter, whatever sex the child should prove to have. Miss Betty was a bit dumpy in shape, so she didn't have to hide away the way a slimmer woman would have had to. Mr. Trent was in a fair rage. He felt the fact that Miss Betty had disgraced herself was a reflection on him.

"Well now, I attended the birth and I was glad it was an easy one, for I felt poor Miss Betty had enough to worry her. It was a lovely baby. She doted on it. She loved that little boy with her whole heart and soul. But Mr. Trent told her he had bought a house up in Sutherland and a flat for Miss Betty and Miss Angela in London. She was to go to London right away and forget about the child. She was to forget it was her own. He had already engaged a nanny. He made her swear to keep quiet about it. He said if she ever told anyone, he would hand the boy back to her and then make sure she never had a penny to support him.

"Miss Betty was weak in spirit after the childbirth, the way mothers are, and she agreed, but she cried something dreadful until I was glad to see her go. I thought she would upset the baby by clutching him and crying over him the way she did. More tea?"

"And did he legally adopt the boy?"

"No, I don't think so. Miss Betty said, what about the birth certificate? He'd find out when he saw his birth certificate. Mr. Trent said there was no need for him ever to see it. He would arrange things like the boy's school and his first passport and things like that. So I don't think he really adopted him.

"I called round to see the baby after Miss Betty had gone and just before Mr. Trent was moving up north. It was a lovely baby and the nanny was very efficient. English, she was, but I can't recall her name. But Miss Betty stuck in my mind. She was crazy about that baby of hers. Crazy, she was."

They finally managed to escape after having made sure she had nothing left to tell them.

"Drive on and park somewhere quiet," ordered Hamish. "We need to think."

Priscilla obediently drove out of Perth and eventually pulled into a parking place on the A9.

"We've got it at last," said Hamish. "We've got the Why. We need the How. Betty Trent is not a big strapping woman like her sister. How could she get the old man into the wardrobe? Where are my notes? Let me think."

He flicked through them impatiently. "Here we are. The night of the murder, she was seen speaking to him. What could she have said? Let me think. I am Betty Trent. I worship my son from afar. I may just have been told that day that he is to inherit nothing. I am mad with rage. My brain is working double time with rage. I get the knife and substitute the blade of the boning knife in the shaft." Hamish fell silent.

Priscilla sat and watched him. He suddenly struck his brow. "Of course!" cried Hamish. "Listen to this, Priscilla. It's easy. Old Trent must have been mad at Titchy Gold for having accused him of ruining her dresses. Say Betty goes up to him. Say she praises him for that joke with the dummy in the wardrobe. Say she says she has an even better idea. What if Dad were to hide himself in the wardrobe with a monster mask on? That would frighten her out of her wits. Trent steps into the wardrobe. Instead of handing him the knife, Betty lets him have it."

"Wait a bit," said Priscilla. "Betty's a small woman. It was a direct blow."

"Damn!" He rubbed his red hair in agitation. "She could have stood on a chair."

"Why?"

"I know. To help him on with the mask...something like that. He turns round in the wardrobe, she ties the strings. He turns to face her. She stabs him and slams the door shut and the door must have kept him propped upright. It's a huge wardrobe but a shallow one and the door is heavy with that great mirror on it."

"And Titchy? Why Titchy?"

"Because I think Betty's mind was already turned by the first murder. Titchy had turned her beloved son down flat. So she takes a cup of chocolate laced with sleeping pills in to Titchy. 'Drink it up like a good girl. It'll make you sleep.'"

"And would Titchy just meekly have done that?"

"I think for all her faults, Titchy would have been disarmed by a show of kindness from one of the ladies of the house. Yes, I think that's the way it was."

"An awfully long shot, Hamish. How are you going to prove it?"

"She's off balance. I'll just tell her how she did it and see if she cracks."

"She may not."

"I'll have the others there."

Priscilla laughed. "Great detective gathers suspects in the library?"

He grinned. "It's just that it might be amazing what some of the others might remember about Betty if they hear her accused of murder." His grin faded. "I hate Andrew Trent. I think he was damned lucky to have lived so long and then to die from a nice clean knife stab. He deserved worse. He's the real murderer in that, by his actions, he created a murderess out of his daughter."

"It's getting late," said Priscilla. "We won't be back till midnight."

"I'll go up in the morning," said Hamish. "Betty's killing days are over. There's nothing that can happen before tomorrow."

"I could kill you," said Jan, glaring at Melissa.

They were all sitting round the dinner table.

"Why do you want to kill her?" asked Charles.

"Because she has talked my gullible son out of giving me any money."

"That's not true, Mother," protested Paul. "We have agreed to give you some money, but not all. You'll find yourself very comfortably off."

"I wouldn't mind," said Jan, "if the girl were really in love with you. But it's your money she wants."

"Is that true?" Betty asked Melissa.

"No, of course not," said Melissa, blushing and angry. "I would marry Paul if he didn't have a penny."

"There you are, Mother," said Paul. "That's the sort of woman you could never understand. Melissa loves me. Damn it. I'll prove it. You can have all the money. All I want is Melissa."

Melissa stomach felt as if she had just been

dropped from a very great height without a parachute. Oh, dear thyme-scented villa on the Mediterranean, dear Costas and Juanita—gone forever. She and Paul would work and scrimp and save for the rest of their lives. The fact that both of them earned very good salaries did not occur to her. What was a very good salary compared to millions? And what of all those clothes she had been studying in a copy of *Vogue*? In her mind's eye, a white Rolls Royce purred along the coast towards that villa carrying, not her, but Jan, selfish, greedy, clutching Jan.

Melissa raised her eyes and looked at Jan, who was sitting next to Paul. One of her bony beringed hands was fondly caressing Paul's sleeve and Paul was giving her a myopic, doting look. Melissa had not been a virgin when she had gone to bed with Paul that day. She'd had one previous affair and one one-night stand. But now she felt, made unreasonable by fury, that Paul had seduced *her* with promises of money. He had *used* her. She pushed back her chair and got shakily to her feet.

"You never meant to let me have any money," she shouted at Paul. "All the time you meant to give it to Mummy dearest. Well, I'm not going to marry anyone with an Oedipus complex. Stuff you and stuff your bloody mother."

She slammed out and ran to her room and threw herself face down on the bed and cried her eyes out. After a while, she grew calmer. If anyone had ever told her that the very prospect of a lot of money would drive her mad with greed and dreams, thought Melissa, sitting up and wiping her eyes, she would not have believed it.

Down in the dining-room, Charles was returning to the topic of Melissa. "I thought her a nice little thing." he said. "I wouldn't have thought money would have meant that much to her."

"What about Titchy?" demanded Betty.

"I suppose so," said Charles ruefully. "But Titchy was different. She had an insecure, unstable sort of life. Now Melissa has a brain and a good job. Come to think of it, I rather fancy her myself, if you must know. I think you'll find, Paul, that she didn't mean a word of it. Girls don't like chaps who are too tied to their mother's apron-strings, not that I would know anything about that personally."

"I'm sorry for Paul," said Betty. "I think he's well rid of Melissa. She reminds me of Titchy with that tarty hair."

"I wish you would all keep your noses out of my business," shouted Paul. "For Christ's sake! One of us is a murderer. I thought that would be enough to occupy your minds."

He walked out, leaving the rest of them looking at each other.

"Yes, but we can't think of that every minute of

the day," said Charles at last. "The police are coming again tomorrow and then we should all be free to go our separate ways. I cannot tell you, Betty, Angela, and Jeffrey, how deeply moved I am by your generosity."

"What's this?" demanded Jan, her voice shrill.

"Oh, Lor'," said Charles. "Well, you'll know soon enough. Betty, Angela, and Jeffrey are going to make over a big chunk each of their fortunes to me."

"Why?" demanded Jan, aghast.

"Because, precious one," sneered her husband, "it's only fair. He should have got the lot, you know."

"You fool," hissed Jan. "You bloody old fool." She stormed out.

"Dear me," said Charles, raising his eyebrows, "I hope the ones of us left can pass the rest of the evening in peace and tranquillity. How is Jan getting back to London, by the way? You drove her up, Jeffrey."

"I'll drive her back," said Jeffrey. "We're still married."

"I'll never understand you," said Charles in amazement. "You spit hate at each other and yet you continue to share the same bed, and now you're driving her back. I owe you a lot, Jeffrey. I'll escort her if you like."

"No, it's all right," said Jeffrey. "She can't frighten me any more. Funny, that. I've been married for years to a woman who frightened me."

*   *   *

Paul was sitting beside Melissa on her bed, holding her hand. "You can't mean you only wanted the money," he was saying.

"Not at first," said Melissa drearily, "but then the prospect of it all went to my head. So good luck to you and Mother dear. I hope you will be very happy."

"I didn't mean it," said Paul quietly. "I only wanted to show them you weren't mercenary. I agree it would be foolish not to enjoy ourselves." His hand caressed the soft pink feathers of her hair. She shivered under his touch. Just before he had said that, she had begun to feel like her own woman again. But the dreams were rushing back in, the clothes, the villa, the servants, the old farmhouse...She gave a groan. "Go away, Paul, and let me think," she said. "I can't think straight living in this house."

He got up reluctantly. "Won't you let me stay with you?"

"Not tonight," said Melissa. "With luck, we'll be allowed to leave tomorrow. I'll know what I want as soon as I'm away from here."

When Paul had left, Melissa washed and undressed and settled down and tried to sleep, tried to banish all those rosy, those wealthy dreams, but they came thick and fast.

Paul had been down to the kitchen for a cup of coffee. He met Betty on the stairs. "You are well out of that engagement, young man," she said.

"Oh, I don't think so," he said cheerfully. "In fact, I'm pretty sure it's back on again."

"Why? Did you tell her you were keeping the money?"

"Well, yes, some of it. But she's not mercenary."

Melissa was just drifting off to sleep when she heard someone entering her room. She had forgotten to lock the door! She sat up in alarm and then relaxed as she saw the dumpy figure of Betty Trent silhouetted against the light from the corridor.

"You've had a horrid evening," said Betty, approaching. "I've brought you a nice glass of hot milk and I want you to drink it all up."

"Oh, thank you." Melissa's eyes filled with tears at this unexpected piece of kindness.

"Think nothing of it," said Betty gently, and she went out and closed the door.

Chapter Eight

So, at last I was going to America! Really, really going, at last! The boundaries burst. The arch of heaven soared. A million suns shone out for every star. The winds rushed in from outer space, roaring in my ears, "America! America!"

—Mary Antin

One by one the guests at Arrat House shuffled down to the library, too anxious to protest at having been roused from their beds so early. All Enrico had told them was that they had been summoned by Constable Macbeth.

"What's it all in aid of?" asked Charles. "And where's Melissa?"

"Enrico says she's asleep and the copper says he doesn't need her," said Jeffrey.

"I don't like the sound of that." Charles wrapped his dressing-gown more tightly about him. "I had a hope, you know, that we were all going to be told to go home."

"Fat chance," remarked Angela bitterly. "Dragging us down here at dawn."

"It's nine in the morning," pointed out Jan. "Oh, I hear cars arriving. Here come the bloody reinforcements."

Hamish Macbeth was waiting on the steps of Arrat House as Blair and his detectives arrived.

"As I told you on the phone, I want you to listen to what I have to say to them," said Hamish, "and I think I'll find your murderer for you."

Blair thanked his stars that Daviot wasn't going to be present. If Hamish made a fool of himself, then he would have all the pleasure of telling Daviot about it. If Hamish solved the murders, then, with any luck, he could claim the success as his own.

Everyone looked up nervously as Hamish, the detectives and two policemen filed into the library.

"Quite a crowd," said Charles amiably.

"Constable Macbeth has something tae say tae ye," said Blair, unable to keep a jeering note out of his voice as Hamish stood in front of the fireplace and faced them all.

"The difficulty in solving this murder was always lack o' motive," began Hamish. "You all, for various reasons, but mostly mercenary, wanted Andrew Trent dead. But one of you had the most powerful motive of all—mother love."

With the exception of Betty, who was knitting furiously, they all looked at Jan.

"No, not Mrs. Jeffrey Trent," said Hamish. "Miss Betty Trent."

Angela's mouth fell open. Betty continued to knit.

"Betty Trent gave birth to Charles in Perth twenty-eight years ago."

"Oh, God," said Charles.

"Angela Trent was abroad for a long time. She did not know of the pregnancy. Andrew Trent did. He was appalled. He considered it a terrible scandal. He arranged for a midwife to deliver the baby and Betty was kept indoors before the birth so that no one would guess her condition. When the baby was born, he sold the house in Perth, bought Arrat House, and a flat in London for Betty and her sister."

"But we had always been asking him if we could live in London," protested Angela. "Betty wrote and told me she had finally persuaded him. Betty would have told me if she were pregnant!"

All looked at Betty, but she knitted on.

"I think you will find from Charles Trent's birth certificate that Betty is his mother, father unknown. He was never adopted. Betty had to suffer seeing her father's indifferent treatment of the boy, not to mention inflicting some of his terrible jokes on the child. But if she told Charles she was his mother, then not only would she be penniless but her son would inherit nothing. I believe that is what she *was* told.

"The way she murdered Andrew Trent was like this. I think Andrew may have told her that he was going to leave Charles nothing. She had a great idea. She prepared the knife and then suggested to Andrew—who must have been furious with Titchy for having been accused by her of ruining those dresses—that instead of a dummy in Titchy's wardrobe, why did he not hide there himself? And that's the way she did it.

"Titchy Gold was not going to marry Charles, and Betty poisoned her with an overdose."

"Wait a bit," interrupted Detective Jimmy Anderson. "Thon blow to the auld man's chest was direct. I mean he must have been struck by someone of the same height if he was killed in the wardrobe."

"I've considered that," said Hamish, beginning to think bleakly that speculation was piling on speculation in his account of how the murder had taken place. "She would stand on a chair, once Andrew Trent was up in the wardrobe, and tie the mask on for him. When he turned round, she stabbed him."

All looked at Betty, except Charles, who had his hands over his face.

Upstairs in her bedroom, Melissa struggled awake, yawned and looked at the clock. She got out of bed, noticing, as she did so, the glass of milk by the bedside. She had only sipped a little bit of it before deciding she had never in the past liked hot milk and nothing had changed. A skin was lying on top of the now cold milk and she shuddered in distaste before taking the glass into the bathroom and pouring the contents down the toilet. Then she washed the glass clean under the hot tap.

She felt much better than she had done for days. It was all very simple. She was not going to marry Paul. To get rid of all those silly dreams of wealth was like coming out of a nightmare. She would leave this terrible place and return briefly to her job while she found another as far away from Paul Sinclair as possible.

Melissa searched through her small stock of clothes for something to wear. There was a long white dress from her university days when it was fashionable to wear long skirts with bare feet. She put it on as if donning an old and comfortable identity. Cheered and feeling defiant, she went back to the bathroom and applied dead-white make-up to her face and purple eye-shadow to her eyes.

She wandered downstairs. No one was about. She opened the front door and looked out. The day was dark and miserable, with low clouds flying over the mountains above the house. She saw the police cars outside and she also saw Hamish Macbeth's white Land Rover. Her heart lifted. She would tell Hamish all about it. The detectives must be in the library. But was Hamish there? She would go outside and look in at the library window ... just to see.

*   *   *

Betty put down her knitting and spoke at last. Her voice was steady and calm. "I admit Charles is my son," she said. She looked at him, her eyes blazing with love and affection, but he still had his face buried in his hands. "But as to the rest, it is pure fantasy, Constable. Where is your proof?"

"Aye," said Blair, rubbing his fat hands. "How are ye going to prove it, Macbeth?"

Hamish felt like a fool. He had gone about it the wrong way. Perhaps he should have got Betty on her own and bullied her, as Blair would have done, suggested that he had concrete evidence, lied, anything to break her.

Betty gave him a little smile and picked up her knitting. As she did so, she looked at the window and then turned quite white. Her hands shook and the knitting dropped to the floor and a ball of that bright magenta wool that Priscilla had bought her rolled to Charles's feet.

Hamish followed her gaze.

Melissa Clarke was framed in the window against the darkness of the day outside. Her white face appeared to float and the wind blew her dress about her.

"Go away," screamed Betty suddenly. "Go away. I'm sorry now. I'm sorry. He deserved to die. They all deserved to die."

In a flat voice, Hamish cautioned her. Then he said

to the others, "You can all leave." But Betty wailed, "No, Charles must hear. I did it for him." Nobody moved. Melissa had disappeared. The wind howled outside. Betty dabbed at her mouth with a handkerchief.

"It was worse than that. He told me that he had left everything to Charles in his will, but that he had changed his mind. He said he was going to phone the lawyers on the following day and change the will. He said Charles was no good. He enjoyed telling me. He was laughing. I'd long dreamt of killing him. I fixed the knife just like you said. When Titchy accused him of ruining her frocks, I knew he was angry with her. So I went up to him and suggested he frighten her to get even. He liked that. He climbed into the wardrobe, giggling like a schoolboy. 'The mask,' I said. 'You've forgotten the mask.' 'No, I haven't,' he said, and drew one of those plastic monster masks from his pocket. 'I'll put it on for you,' I said, and as he was standing up in the wardrobe, I brought forward a chair and stood on that. I tied the mask. He turned around and grinned at me. 'Give me the knife, Betty,' he said. So I gave it to him. 'Here you are, you old bastard,' I said, and I plunged the knife into his chest and slammed the door. I couldn't believe what I'd done. I saw myself reflected in the glass of the door. I looked... ordinary."

"And Titchy?" prompted Hamish gently.

"She was dumping Charles because he hadn't any money and all because Dad had had the final laugh. He never meant to leave anything to Charles at all.

So I took the tablets out of Jeffrey's cabinet and took them to her."

"And Melissa?" asked Hamish. "Why Melissa?"

Jan screamed and Paul started up. "Not Melissa!" he shouted. "We saw her at the window."

"That was her ghost," explained Betty with mad patience. "I knew then that I must confess or they would all come back to haunt me. It worked. I confessed and she went away. You see, Charles said he fancied her and she is mercenary, just like Titchy. Angela and Jeffrey and I were giving Charles a share of our money. I did not want Melissa to get it, so she had to die, too. Paul said the engagement was back on but I did not believe him. She was after Charles."

"How did you kill her?" asked Hamish.

"I had those sleeping tablets left. I only used half the bottle to kill Titchy. I had sewn the rest into a hem of my dress. I had crushed the bottle to powder and put the powder into one of those lavender sachets in my underwear drawer. So I took Melissa a glass of milk last night." She turned to Charles. "She wouldn't feel a thing, you know. I'm glad it's all over. Oh, my dear son, come to Mummy." She held out her short plump arms.

With a cry of horror, Charles ran from the room.

Blair turned to Hamish as Betty was being ushered into one of the police cars and said, "Man, you were lucky. Not a shred of proof."

"But I solved your case for you," said Hamish, "so if you don't want me to take the credit, I suggest you arrange with Strathbane to get central heating put in the police station at Lochdubh."

Blair grinned. "Oh, no, you don't, you conniving bastard. Daviot wisnae here. She confessed. That's all there is tae it. 'Bye, 'bye, Macbeth. See you around."

In a fury, Hamish watched him go. One photographer, more alert than the rest at the gate, had spotted Betty being taken to the police car through his telescopic lens and had started clicking his camera, which alerted the others. As Blair's car swept by the press, they all scrambled for their own to pursue him to Strathbane.

Hamish turned and went indoors, nearly colliding with Enrico. "May I fetch you some refreshment, Constable?" asked Enrico.

"No," said Hamish. "Where are they all?"

"Mrs. Jeffrey is lying down. Her son has gone up to see how she is. The rest are in the drawing-room."

Hamish went into the drawing-room. Charles was huddled in a chair. Angela was sitting on the arm of it with her arm round his shoulders. Jeffrey was leaning forward, looking at Charles with concern, and Melissa was hovering by the window. Melissa looked a mess. Blair had berated her for washing out that glass. She had burst into tears, so that purple eye-shadow had run down in purple rivulets over her white make-up.

"Oh, Hamish," she cried, running to him. "Is it really all over? Did she really do it?"

"Aye," said Hamish, removing his peaked cap and sitting down. "She really did." He looked across at Charles. "Don't take it too hard," he said. "Andrew Trent's cruelty turned your mother's mind. I doubt if she's fit to stand trial."

"Just what Jeffrey and I have been telling him," said Angela robustly. "I never liked Betty, but we were sort of bound together in a way, both being spinsters, both dependent on Dad for our money. But then a lot of women don't like their sisters. Have you any idea who Charles's father is?"

"She refused to say," said Hamish, "and to my mind it's chust as well. Charles has had enough shocks for one day."

"Our offer of money to you still stands," said Jeffrey to Charles. "Betty cannot inherit through crime, so her share will come to the rest of us. Angela and I will see you're all right, boy."

Charles raised an anguished face. "What bothers me is that I don't feel a thing," he said. "I mean, I'm shocked by everything, but I cannot think of Betty Trent as my mother. I don't feel a thing for her."

"Don't let it worry you," said Hamish. "You're in shock."

"Oh, Hamish, I must talk to you," said Melissa. "I'm not going to marry Paul."

"Well, that's a sensible decision." Hamish got up to go.

"I mean, can I have a word with you outside?" begged Melissa.

"I'm still on duty," said Hamish. "I've got things to do."

Melissa sat down mournfully after he had left. She had hoped he would want to talk to her. After all, she herself had nearly been murdered.

"Is there anything we can do for you?" Angela was asking Charles.

He gave a bleak smile. "Nothing more than you have done. You and Jeffrey have been so kind. Oh, I know. Could you lend me your car, Jeffrey? I would like to drive away from here for a bit and get some fresh air."

Jeffrey handed him the car keys. "Be my guest."

Charles took the keys and stood up and walked to the door. "Come on, Melissa," he said. "You'd probably like to get out of here as well." He walked off and Melissa scrambled after him.

"It's odd," said Jeffrey to Angela. "I feel the nightmare is over. I don't think Betty will ever stand trial. I don't even hate Jan any more."

"But you'll leave her?"

"Oh, yes, I'll leave her. What about you, Angela? What will you do?"

"When the money comes in, I'll travel," said Angela. "Sunny countries, Jeffrey, white beaches, foreign people."

"That's the ticket," he said with a grin.

"And I'll be there for Charles if he needs me."

Jeffrey sighed. "He'll get over it quicker than we will, Angela. He never knew Betty as his mother. I think with our money, he'll lead the dilettante life he's always wanted, never work again, and be perfectly happy."

"Must you drive so fast?" shouted Melissa. Charles slowed the car to a halt and then switched off the engine. He had stopped on a rise and below them stretched acres of wind-swept moorland and tall pillared mountains. Clouds rushed overhead and the wind sang mournfully through the heather. "The land that God forgot," said Charles.

"What will you do?" asked Melissa.

"Oh, I'll travel the way I've always wanted to travel," said Charles. "The best cure I can think of is to get right out of Britain. I'll go to New York, stay at the Plaza, and then, after a few weeks, I'll buy a car and drive right across America."

"Won't you want to see your mother?"

"No point," he said. He handed her a handkerchief. "Here. Scrub your face. You look like a clown. All your make-up's run."

"It's not my fault," said Melissa, rubbing her face and looking ruefully at the mess on the handkerchief. "I got such a fright when I heard she'd tried to murder me that I couldn't stop crying."

"Well, by all that's holy." Charles fished a flask out of the glove compartment. He unscrewed the top. "Brandy." He drank some and passed the flask to Melissa, who took a great gulp. "Easy now," he admonished. "Fair shares.

"You didn't see my mother before she was taken out," he went on. "Her eyes were completely blank. She didn't even know who I was. She'll never go to trial. God, all those years and I didn't know. I remember now when I was small, she once took me on her lap and she was kissing and hugging me and old Andrew walked in. I can't call him Father. I never really could. He walked in and said in a nasty voice, 'Don't ever let me catch you doing that again.' Horrible man."

They finished the brandy. Charles stretched a lazy arm around Melissa's shoulders. "D'you know what I feel like doing now? Making love."

"To me?" Melissa looked at him tipsily.

"Who else?" He gathered her close and kissed her. His kiss was soothing, warm and friendly. One kiss led to another, and another somehow led to both of them in the back seat making cramped but energetic love.

Melissa didn't feel ashamed or used. She would never see him again. They would go their separate ways.

"What are you going to do now?" he asked lazily. "Are you a dedicated scientist?"

"I thought I was," said Melissa. "I'll know when I get back. But Paul will be there. I'd better find another job."

He ruffled her short hair. "Come with me to the States."

"What! Just like that?"

"Why not? Have you got family?"

"Yes, my mum and dad. I don't live with them. I've got my own flat."

"Okay, we'll drop in on Mum and Dad and then we'll be off."

Melissa began to laugh. "Silly, you haven't any money yet."

"But I will have, the minute Jeffrey and Angela phone the lawyers. I'll ask the lawyers for a great whacking advance. Think of it. Oodles of money and nothing else to do but have fun. I say, we can clear off today. I can't stand another night at Arrat House."

"But Paul will be furious."

"You don't need to see him or anyone. I'll say good-bye to Jeffrey and Angela and tell them to keep quiet about it. We won't even pack. We'll just go off as if we're going into the village for a stroll and then call a cab."

Melissa twisted her head and looked up at him, at his handsome face. She couldn't leave with him. She didn't know him. Mind you, her working-class background wouldn't bother Charles. She instinctively knew he wouldn't particularly notice it. But she couldn't really ...

"Let's get to know each other better," said Melissa firmly. "Then I'll know it's you I want and not your money!"

Hamish Macbeth was sitting in the village café with Priscilla. He had previously arranged to meet her there. He told her all about the confrontation and Betty's confession, ending with, "I'll neffer do that again."

"What?" asked Priscilla, guessing by the sudden sibilancy of his Highland accent that he was really upset.

"I will neffer again try tae frighten a confession out o' someone. Next time I will hae the proof, rock-solid proof. If Melissa hadnae appeared at the window complete wi' punk make-up, I might still ha' been waiting for a confession, and that scunner Blair laughing at me. And do you know what Blair has done?"

"I should guess, as you told me Daviot wasn't there, that he is going to take all the credit," said Priscilla. "So what's new? You usually let him."

"Aye, but this time I wass going to bargain. I wass going to haff the central heating put in at the police station."

"Maybe that will teach you to be a little more ambitious in future, Hamish Macbeth."

"Oh, aye?" said Hamish. "And end up in Strathbane? You wouldnae see me. Would you miss me, Priscilla?"

"Of course I would. But I would be happy to see you getting on. How is Charles Trent taking it? He must be devastated."

"I think he'll get over it quick. He's getting money from Jeffrey and Angela. The man's a born hedonist."

"You underrate him," said Priscilla, "just because he's handsome."

"Regretting you didn't go for dinner with him?"

"Madly," said Priscilla crossly. "I'd better get back to Lochdubh. What about you?"

"I'll call at Arrat House and pick up the Land Rover and follow you."

They emerged from the café together and then stood staring down the street. Charles and Melissa were emerging from the pub. A taxi was waiting for them. They were very tipsy and laughing and giggling. Charles kissed Melissa full on the mouth and then they both got into the taxi.

"Shattered, isn't he?" said Hamish.

"How could it all happen just like that?" marvelled Priscilla.

"Isn't that the way it's supposed to happen?" asked Hamish.

She avoided his eyes. "My car's here. I'll run you to Arrat House."

Priscilla waited outside while Hamish went in to say good-bye. He emerged after ten minutes, followed by Enrico. The Spaniard said something to Hamish and handed him a small parcel.

Then Hamish came up to Priscilla's car. "What was that?" she asked.

"A wee present," said Hamish with a grin. "lead the way home, Priscilla, and I'll give you a police escort."

That evening at police headquarters in Strathbane, Jimmy Anderson held the phone out to Blair. "It's Hamish Macbeth," he said.

Blair laughed. "Whit does our local yokel want now?" he asked. He took the phone.

"Whit dae ye want, laddie?"

"Central heating," said Hamish.

"Och, away and bile yer heid, ye daft pillock."

"Pity if you refuse to help." Hamish's voice sounded amused. "By the way, I got a farewell present from Enrico at Arrat House. That tape."

"Wipe it out, man," howled Blair.

"Aye, that I will. After."

"After whit?"

"After I get the central heating," said Hamish gently and replaced the receiver.

Chapter One

Where'er you walk cool gales shall fan the glade;
Trees, where you sit, shall crowd into a shade;
Where'er you tread, the blushing flow'rs shall rise,
And all things flourish where you turn your eyes.

—Alexander Pope

It is a well-known fact that just when a man reaches his early thirties and thinks he is past love, that is when love turns the corner and knocks the feet from under him.

That was what was about to happen to Police Sergeant Macbeth. But on a particularly fine sunny day when the mountains of Sutherland in the northwest of Scotland stood up blue against the even bluer sky and not a ripple moved on the surface of the sea loch in front of the village of Lochdubh, he was blissfully unaware of what the fates had in store for him.

The only irritation in his life was the appointment

of a constable to assist him, police headquarters in Strathbane having discovered that the small police station in Lochdubh was an excellent way of getting rid of the deadbeats. Constable Dick Fraser was marking time until his retirement. He was a lazy grey-haired man, but he had an amiable disposition, and since he arrived in Lochdubh a month ago, there had been no crime at all which suited him very well.

Hamish learned that there was a relative newcomer, an elderly widow called Mrs. Colchester, who had bought an old hunting box some miles outside Braikie. During the winter, he had meant to call on her, but somehow the days and months had slipped past.

Dick was asleep in a deck chair in the front garden, his breath causing his grey moustache to rise and fall.

"Get up!" snapped Hamish.

Dick's pale blue eyes slowly opened. He struggled out of the deck chair and stood up. Most of his weight was concentrated on a beer belly and he was quite short for a policeman and dwarfed by Hamish who was over six feet tall.

"What's up?" he asked sleepily.

"We're going to call on a newcomer, a Mrs. Colchester."

"Someone killed the old bitch?" asked Dick.

"Why do you say that?"

"I heard gossip she's considered poison. Bad, nasty mouth on her and she's got two grandchildren from hell living with her. Also, she's right fed up because Lord Growther, who used to own the place, left Buchan's Wood, the prettiest part of the estate to the town of Braikie. Now, some lass on Braikie council has been appointed the council director of tourism and the environment and she's been running tours to the wood. She's renamed it the Fairy Glen."

"Where on earth did you pick up all this gossip?" marvelled Hamish. "You hardly move."

"When you're out, people stop by the hedge for a wee chat. It does not, surely, take the two of us to go there."

"Oh, yes it does, you lazy moron. Brush down your uniform. It's covered in biscuit crumbs, and let's get moving."

The house which Mrs. Colchester had bought lay six miles to the north of Braikie. It was an unprepossessing place at the end of a long drive, being built of grey granite without any creepers to soften its harsh square structure.

The doorbell was an old-fashioned one set into the stone. Hamish rang it. They waited a long time until they heard shuffling footsteps approach from the other side of the door. The woman who answered it was squat and bent, leaning on two sticks and peering up at them out of sharp black eyes from under a heavy fringe of wiry grey hair.

"Mrs. Colchester?" asked Hamish.

"Yes, what is it? Is it those grandchildren of mine again?"

"No, no," said Hamish soothingly, removing his peaked cap and nudging Dick to do the same. "Just a wee social call."

"You may as well come in. But make it short." Her accent had been anglicised but still held some lilting traces of a highland accent. Somewhere in the Hebrides, guessed Hamish.

She led them into a large square hall patterned with black and white tiles. It was wood panelled. There was a hard chair by the door and a side table against one wall. Apart from those items, there wasn't any other furniture and no paintings decorated the walls.

"Drawing room's on the first floor," said Mrs. Colchester. She waddled across the hall to where a stair lift had been built. She climbed in, fastened a seat belt, and said, "Follow me."

The stair lift went on and up, smoothly and efficiently, stopping on the first-floor landing. Light flooded down from a blue glass cupola up on the roof. She extricated herself from the stair lift and led them into a large drawing room.

Hamish looked around, wondering if she had bought the furnishings along with the house. There were several grimy landscapes of Scottish scenes decorating the walls. The furniture was Victorian, heavy, solid and intricately carved. A large silver-framed mirror dominated the marble mantelpiece. There were several round tables, dotted here and there, small islands on a sea of a rose-patterned carpet, bleached pale by the sunlight.

From the window, Hamish could see Buchan's Wood. A tour bus drove up to a newly built clearing which served as a car park and began to dislodge passengers. He swung round.

"I believe you are upset that Buchan's Wood, or the Fairy Glen as I understand it has been renamed, is not a part of your estate."

"Oh, sit down and stop poking about," said Mrs. Colchester. "Do you dye your hair?"

Hamish's hair was flaming red in a patch of sunlight. "No," he said crossly.

"Well, as to your question, I was upset at first but then that Mary Leinster called on me. She persuaded me that the beauty of the place should be shown to as many people as possible. She has the second sight, you know."

"A lot of people claim to have that gift," said Hamish cautiously.

"Oh, but she is the real thing. I have my two grandchildren staying with me for the school holidays. Charles is twelve and Olivia sixteen. Mary called on me last week and said Charles was in peril because he was going to fall into the pool below the falls. I know he can't swim. I didn't believe her but two days later Charles did fall in and, if it hadn't been for one of the tourists who dived in and rescued him, he would have been drowned."

"I think we'll take a look at the place," said Hamish.

"Go ahead. Are you as stupid as you look?"

Hamish blinked. Then he rallied and said, "Are you as rude and nasty as you appear?"

"Get out of here," she snapped, "and take that fat fool with you. And don't come back."

"After such a warm welcome," said Hamish sweetly, "it will be right hard for me to stay away. Come along, Dick."

As they walked down the stairs to the hall, they found two children at the bottom of the stairs surveying them.

"I gather you must be Charles and Olivia," said Hamish.

"Cut the crap," said Charles. "Is the old bat dead yet?"

"She is very much alive," said Hamish coldly.

"Christ, she'll live forever," said Olivia gloomily.

Hamish sat down on the bottom step and surveyed them curiously. Charles was small and thin with a shock of fair, almost white, hair and flat grey eyes. His sister was a slightly taller version with the same colour of hair and eyes. Both had very white skin and thin pale lips and long thin noses.

"Why do you want your grandmother dead?" he asked.

"Because our parents say our school fees are too

much and they are threatening to send us to the local comprehensive where we'll be stuck with morons and chavs. If granny dies, they get the money."

"You're English?"

"Yeah, from London," said Olivia. "You know, where real people live, instead of, like, Moronsville up here."

The floorboards above them creaked. "Here she comes," said Charles. Both children scampered out the open door and disappeared down the drive.

"Let's go," urged Hamish. "A little o' Granny Colchester goes a long way."

"I'm hungry," complained Dick. "She could at least have offered us something."

"That old cow? Forget it. Let's have a look at this wood."

Groaning, Dick heaved his bulk into the passenger seat of the police Land Rover. "You'll need to feed your beasties anyway," said Dick. Hamish had two pets, a mongrel called Lugs and a wild cat called Sonsie. Hamish had left them behind at the police station. To Hamish's relief, both animals seemed fond of Dick.

"Just a quick look," said Hamish, "and then I'd like to visit this Mary Leinster. I mean, think how easy it would be to get someone to shove that child in the pool and then get a friend on hand to save the boy. Second sight confirmed. No more arguments about the use of the wood from granny."

They parked beside the tour bus. Hamish noticed

what looked like a gift shop was under construction. Mrs. Timoty, an old-age pensioner from Braikie, stood at the entrance to the wood beside a turnstile. "That'll be three pounds each," she said, "and five pounds for the car."

"This is police business," said Hamish, walking past her. They followed a pokerwork sign with the legend Fairy Glen.

Sutherland is not famous for trees because of the frequent Atlantic gales which leave the landscape dotted with poor bent over apologies for trees. But there are a few beautiful glens and waterfalls, sheltered from the brutality of the wind.

Because of the proximity of the gulf stream, former Scottish gardeners had been able to plant rare varieties of trees and shrubs. A gravelled path twisted its way among the beauty of overhanging trees and great bushes of fuchsia. They stood aside to let the tourists make their way back to their bus.

Hamish, followed by Dick, came to a rustic bridge spanning the pool. The roar of the waterfall, which descended into the pool, filled their ears, and little rainbows danced in shafts of sunlight.

"My, but it's rare bonnie," said Dick.

"Shh!" said Hamish. "Look at that!"

A kingfisher dived into the pool and rose again, a fish in its beak, its sapphire blue wings flashing. It disappeared under the trailing branches of a weeping willow and disappeared.

Large flat grey stones surrounded the pool. Hamish guessed the boy must have been playing on one of them when he was pushed in. If he had been on the bridge with the sightseers, then someone would have noticed. The boy would need to have been lifted bodily over the railing.

Hamish had a longing, just to stay there, drinking in the peace of the place. But he was becoming curious about this Mary Leinster.

"I think we should go to the town hall in Braikie and visit Miss Leinster," he said. "Did the gossips tell you how Mrs. Colchester got her money?"

"Herself was married to a merchant banker. Before his death, he sold the bank to an American bank and she copped the lot on his death. So the son and daughter, now, that would be a Mr. and Mrs. Palfour, are right cheesed off because they're finding it hard to make ends meet. He's a landscape gardener and owns a nursery, but it's this recession. No one seems to want their gardens landscaped. The kids go to a progressive private school, you know, the kind where they're allowed to express themselves which translates into a lot of four letter words and no work."

Hamish looked at his sidekick with new respect. He knew how valuable gossip was in any investigation. He laughed. "Maybe you're like Poirot, Dick, and sit in your deck chair and exercise your little grey cells. How did you hear this?"

"Mrs. McColl, her what is married to that crofter up the brae at Lochdubh, goes out cleaning and twice a week she and Bertha Dunglass goes up to the house. When Granny gets a letter from her daughter, she reads it aloud and laughs her nasty auld head off."

A cloud passed over the sun. The pool below them grew dark, mirroring the flying clouds overheard. Although it was a windy day, the glen was sheltered.

"Let's go," said Hamish.

Braikie was not very large and would have been considered a fair-sized village in England. The locals did refer to it as "the village," feeling that sounded, well, *classier*.

The town hall was a massive red sandstone building. Mary Leinster had secured an office on the ground floor. They were told she was out but was expected back at any moment. They took seats in the reception area and settled down to wait.

Dick promptly fell asleep. The rumblings of his stomach and his gentle snores sounded out a little symphony.

A small woman walked into the reception area and spoke to the receptionist at the desk and then swung round. "Mr. Macbeth? You wanted to see me?"

Hamish nudged Dick awake and got to his feet. The sun pouring in the open doorway was in his eyes and he could not see her clearly.

"Come through to my office," she said. Her voice had a gentle highland lilt.

She entered a room to the left of the hall and ushered them in. Mary Leinster took her place behind a desk and waved them into two chairs in front of it.

Hamish looked at her in wonderment. She had a heart-shaped face and wide blue eyes fringed by heavy lashes. Her hair was long and curly, strawberry blond, and rioted down to her shoulders. She was wearing a low-cut green blouse of some silky material which showed the tops of two round white breasts.

Mary looked at Hamish and gave a slow smile. She had pink curved lips.

Hamish experienced a sudden breathlessness.

"What has brought Sutherland's famous police officer to see me?" she asked.

Hamish pulled himself together. Dick was gaping at Mary, his mouth open. Hamish leaned across and shut Dick's mouth and glared at him.

"It is about the boy, Charles Palfour," he said. "I believe you haff the second sight." Hamish's accent always became more sibilant when he was excited or upset.

"I don't know if I have or not," said Mary. "I just had this premonition. It came and went in a flash. I saw the boy struggling in the water. I have often seen him playing down on those stones by the pool. So I warned Mrs. Colchester that the boy was not to play there. She didn't believe me. So it happened, ten days ago, just as I had envisaged. Do you believe in the second sight, Mr. Macbeth?"

"Hamish, please."

"Hamish then. I feel we are going to be friends."

"We have a seer in the village of Lochdubh, Angus Macdonald, who claims to have the second sight. You must forgive me, Mary. You see, before I met you I thought it might be a stunt to promote the Fairy Glen."

She gave a charming giggle. "Hamish, the place is extremely popular already." Then she grew serious and leaned her arms on her desk. "With the recession, you know, there's not enough work up here. Because of the popularity of the glen, we have been able to give work to wardens, build a gift shop, and bring money into the economy of the region. Now, you must excuse me. I have a meeting."

Hamish stood up. Dick had fallen asleep. Hamish surreptitiously kicked him on the leg and he awoke with a jerk.

"Here is one of our brochures." Mary handed one to Hamish. On the cover was a very good colour photograph of the kingfisher, rising from the pool, sunlight flashing from the spray on its wings.

Hamish desperately wanted to see her again but she was now holding the door open. He said goodbye and walked sadly out to the police Land Rover. He didn't know anything about her. Had she been wearing a wedding ring? He could not remember.

As he moved off, he said, "I wonder if she's married."

The sleepy source of gossip next to him said, "Yes, she is."

"How do you know that?"

"Oh, a wee bittie talk here and there. Her husband is Tim Leinster. He and his brother are builders. Not much work around these days but I suppose they got the contract to build the gift shop."

"Now that would be right illegal if she's giving contracts out to the nearest and dearest."

"No, it was passed by the council. They're the only builders in Braikie."

"Then why haven't I heard of them?" howled Hamish.

"They only moved up here from Perth last year."

"Why?"

"I suppose they followed Mary when she got the job. Also, they've done a bit of work here and there since they arrived and everyone says they're reasonable and honest."

That's life, thought Hamish gloomily. Romance walks in one minute and walks out the next. Why am I such a failure with women? He thought of how he had nearly proposed marriage to television presenter, Elspeth Grant; how he had once been deeply in love with Priscilla Halburton-Smythe, daughter of the colonel who ran the Tommel Castle Hotel, and how he had been forced to end the engagement because of Priscilla's sexual coldness.

Was he turning out to be one of those sad sacks, always doomed to fall in love with the unattainable?

He mentally pulled himself together. He probably wouldn't see her again.

When he got back to the police station, it was to find an angry message from police headquarters telling him to go directly to Cnothan where two stolen cars had been reported.

Hamish loaded the cat and dog into the back of the Land Rover. Dick was wide awake now and complaining bitterly of hunger.

On the road, they passed a tour bus with the legend Fairy Glen on the front. It seemed to be full of people. He reflected that Mary seemed to be a dab hand at publicity.

Hamish considered Cnothan a sour, unfriendly place, and, although it was on his beat, he visited it as little as possible. One bleak main street led down to a man-made loch. The locals prided themselves on "keeping themselves to themselves."

He knew there was a caravan park and camping area outside the village and headed there. The missing cars were a blue Ford Fiesta and a Peugeot. He checked with the slatternly woman who ran the campsite to check for recent arrivals. She said there were just two, brothers, Angus and Harry McAndrews. Their tent was pitched out at the edge of the campsite.

The two men were seated outside their tent, cooking sausages on a frying pan over a camp stove. They were both skinheads, covered in prison tattoos.

"Whit does the filth want wi' us?" demanded one of them.

"I'm looking for two stolen cars," said Hamish.

"Whit's that got tae dae wi' us?"

Hamish looked around. Next to the brothers' tent was a large bell tent with the front flap tightly closed.

"What's in there?" he asked.

"Naethin tae dae wi' us," said the one who seemed to be the elder.

"Then you won't mind if I have a look."

They both stood up. One reached down and picked up a tyre iron. "Get lost, copper," he snarled.

Hamish reached out and seized the arm holding the tyre iron and twisted it hard. The man let out a yelp of pain and dropped it. His brother tried to run but Dick stuck out a foot and tripped him up. They cuffed both of them. Hamish then looked in the bell tent and found the cars. He charged both of them with theft. He phoned headquarters in Strathbane and was told to stay on guard until a police van arrived to take them away. To make sure the brothers did not try to escape, even though they were handcuffed, Hamish forced them down on the ground and dragged their trousers around their ankles.

He turned round to tell Dick to put the stove out

only to find that Dick had served himself sausages on a paper plate and was busily eating them.

"You're a disgrace," complained Hamish.

"It's not as if they're evidence," said Dick through a mouthful of sausages. "These are rare good. I wonder if they got them locally?"

Back at the police station after what seemed like a long day and having completed all the necessary paperwork, Hamish retreated to the kitchen. From the living room came the noisy sounds of a television game show. He put his head around the living room door and shouted, "Mince and tatties for supper?"

Dick reluctantly lowered the sound, the remote control clutched firmly in one chubby hand. "What's that?"

"I asked you if you wanted mince and tatties for your supper."

"Oh, aye, grand," said Dick.

"I'll call you when it's ready."

Dick threw him a pleading look. "Could I no' just eat my meal in here in front o' the telly? Just the once?"

Hamish thought wryly that Dick looked like a child pleading with a stern parent. "Oh, all right. But don't you start dropping food on the floor!"

Dick smiled and blasted up the sound again.

It wasn't as if the man was deaf, grumbled Hamish

to himself. It was almost as if by jacking up the sound, he could be part of the show itself. "I've spoiled him," said Hamish to Lugs and Sonsie. "I've been happy just to go on as if I'm still on my own. But tomorrow, no more deck chair for Dick. He can come out on the rounds with me. Also, he'd better begin to do his share of the cooking."

He knew Dick was a widower whose wife had died ten years ago. He seemed to have no idea at all of household work and had even on one occasion plaintively asked Hamish to show him how the vacuum cleaner worked.

But, the man was pleasant enough, and it didn't look as if any major crime was ever going to happen again.

The morning would prove Hamish wrong.

He was frying up bacon and eggs while Dick watched a breakfast show on television when the phone in the office rang.

When he answered it, Mary Leinster gasped out, "It's me. Mary. Come quickly. They've hanged him! In the glen," and rang off.

Hamish erupted into the living room and yelled, "Turn that damn thing off. We've got a murder!"

VISIT US ONLINE AT

WWW.HACHETTEBOOKGROUP.COM

FEATURES:

**OPENBOOK BROWSE AND
SEARCH EXCERPTS**

·

AUDIOBOOK EXCERPTS AND PODCASTS

·

AUTHOR ARTICLES AND INTERVIEWS

·

**BESTSELLER AND PUBLISHING
GROUP NEWS**

·

SIGN UP FOR E-NEWSLETTERS

·

**AUTHOR APPEARANCES AND TOUR
INFORMATION**

·

SOCIAL MEDIA FEEDS AND WIDGETS

·

DOWNLOAD FREE APPS

Bookmark Hachette Book Group
@ www.HachetteBookGroup.com